Alan Sillitoe was born in 1928, and left school at fourteen to work in various factories until becoming an air traffic control assistant with the Ministry of Aircraft Production in 1945.

He enlisted in May 1946 into the RAFVR, and spent two years on active service in Malaya as a wireless operator. At the end of 1949 he was invalided out of the service with a hundred per cent disability pension.

He began writing, and lived for six years in France and Spain. His first stories were published in the *Nottinghamshire Weekly Guardian*. In 1958 *Saturday Night and Sunday Morning* was published, and *The Loneliness of the Long Distance Runner*, which won the Hawthornden Prize for literature, came out the following year. Both these books were made into films.

Further works include *Key to the Door*, *The Ragman's Daughter* and *The General* (both also filmed), the *William Posters* trilogy, *A Start in Life*, *Raw Material*, *The Widower's Son*, *The Second Chance* and *The Lost Flying Boat* – as well as several volumes of poetry. His latest books include *Life Goes On*, *Out of the Whirlpool* and *The Open Door*. With his wife, Ruth Fainlight, he divides his time between London and a house in France.

By the same author

ALAN SILLITOE

Last Loves

Paladin
An Imprint of Grafton Books
A Division of HarperCollinsPublishers

Paladin
An imprint of GraftonBooks
A Division of HarperCollins*Publishers*
77–85 Fulham Palace Road,
Hammersmith, London W6 8JB

Published in Paladin 1991
9 8 7 6 5 4 3 2 1

First published in Great Britain by
GraftonBooks 1990

ISBN 0-586-09097-5

Printed in Great Britain by
HarperCollins Manufacturing, Glasgow

Set in Stempel Garamond

For Anne Schlachter

one

In her dreams were many lovers, in her life but few. She never knew who she went to bed with in her dreams, though it didn't much matter because that way she didn't have to remember them, or worry whether they were man, woman or beast. As far as that went they could be friends, family or – she laughed, letting herself into the bath – the fiends of hell. If such was the quality of her dreams, what they were for, then so be it. If they were murky, at least they were rich, and if they were rich she had nothing to complain about, and if she didn't remember them, so much the better, for they would come again, and maybe again and again, until she did remember, if they insisted, and if that was to be the object of her existence, though she hoped it wasn't, because there had to be more to life than unrememberable dreams. And if such dreams didn't come again, because it was for your own good that they did not, then so much the better.

Being unable to remember those undoubtedly thick dreams might only mean there was something of herself she could never entirely – or even remotely – know about, and no one could quarrel with that. Certainly these days she went to bed with somebody or other in her dreams, probably because she had been to bed only with herself for too long. On those occasions when she did go to bed with another person she either didn't dream or, even more rare, remembered them when she did, at least according to a diary she had kept for a few weeks some years ago. And who was she to disbelieve what she had put down in black and white, much as she might now and again want to?

She had stopped filling in the diary, given it up as a bad job because it was too intimidating, too bossy, and hardly the task to impose on herself when work at the office did all that and more. The diary had been given to her by a lover who, she surmised, wanted to keep tabs on what she got up to when he wasn't with her. She once went out of the room and came back to see him looking through it. The notion being confirmed, she froze him out. An affair was an affair, but she was unwilling to be anybody's mistress except her own.

She saved the leatherbound diary, though barely a quarter full, because somebody, even if only a machine, had been put to the trouble of making it, and you don't throw anything into the dustbin that has taken such ingenuity to produce. In any case it looked well among her books in the lounge. And all memories, good, bad or indifferent, were too precious to throw out, because what other evidence did you have to prove that you had lived?

Perhaps she never remembered her dreams because they were always cut off by the alarm clock, bells shattering the dark valley in which murky dalliance was taking place.

The bathroom door was closed and locked, she wouldn't hear the telephone, that more social alarm bell which often pulled her out of daytime dreams, though they at least were less fantastical, and more easily remembered because she had consciously set them going. Scrab the bull terrier was in his basket in the kitchen, and even he – another alarm bell, if you like – by now knew enough not to disturb her during bath time. Tomorrow it would be goodbye for a fortnight, but she doubted that in his murkiest canine dreams he would think she had abandoned him, lavish commons tipped daily into his bowl by the gay man and his boyfriend who lived in the flat upstairs.

Her present lover was the bath, hot water casing her like silk, ritual caresses draining her of passion, as always before a journey, to calm the fibres of her nerves, so as to emerge clean and emphasize herself as she was and had always wanted to be, and not to care overmuch if the aircraft crashed, exploded, burned up, or was flown to some fly-blown desert place by a gang of awful terrorists.

In her daylight dreams were many horrors but – as in her nightscapes when she knew of them – they were never spoken of to anyone. The sudden disintegration of an aircraft was of necessity, she supposed, one which always troubled her the evening before a trip. If four hundred others to go in the Jumbo were having similar misgivings might not their total fear bring on the Act of God to down them all?

She felt a flush of shame that a woman of thirty-six should be apprehensive about flying to Malaysia when she had been on numerous holiday planes before. Perhaps superstition was useful in that the vision of something dreadful happening might be a guarantee that it would not.

She laughed, though not at the faint reflection of her slim pink body in the mirror when she stood up reaching for the towel. Through the condensation she saw a fluffed-out aureole of fair but greying hair above a questioning face which even her smile could not deny. She liked the slim chest and shapely legs, knowing herself to be lithe and fit, and nothing ever wrong except some backache at the start of her periods which she wouldn't, thank God, be having on the trip, because organizing a solicitor's office at least enabled her to plan against inconveniences of that sort.

She could not excise intimations of anxiety, though they could indeed be smiled away on recalling how she invariably got the shakes even on the night before a journey up to Town.

But this time there was a new depth to her fear, unless it was a spiritual uplift to a higher plane of being, neither of which she would particularly like if they made her feel to be anyone less than the normally composed self she took care to show to the world.

All other trips had been pure holiday, a fortnight on a beach in Cyprus or Spain, so that imagining a possible smash had been easier to laugh at. The present journey had been conjured by occasional musings over the years since her parents had died. Coming into her own first flat with those disparate pieces of furniture were boxes of letters and photographs concerning her father who had worked all his life as a public servant in Malaya. The long plan smouldered, that one day she would see some of the places he had written about to her mother.

Right or wrong, she didn't know, nor wanted to at this late stage, since it would do no good. Uncertainty only pumped in more senseless worry, which she didn't like and wasn't made for. She had forced herself to prepare the trip, or something not part of herself had put her up to it, and not knowing even now whether she approved of the idea made her question how far she had been manipulated, a feeling she liked least of all.

Probably the whole thing was the result of some murky dream long ago, a dream which in its insidious way hadn't been by any means unremembered by some part of her mind she would rather not know about, but had deceived her by only pretending to hold back. Such thoughts were too complicated to pursue, and she disliked them, sensing that when we do not know what we dream we sooner or later have to live through such events in real life.

She rarely slept well the night before a trip, and even though the plane didn't leave till late afternoon she assumed that this time it would be the same or maybe worse because, not being a holiday, but an indulgence whose reasoning she would not be able to explain if anyone asked, or if anything went wrong, it filled her with a dread she wished were part of a dream rather than something her perversity had shaped out of reality. At the office she told them that she wanted to go to Malaysia: 'Somewhere different, that's all. I've saved up for it by having no holiday last year. Tidied my garden instead.' She could not admit to going so far on what might be seen as a sentimental whim, though at times it felt as if she were setting up the kind of situation that would have to be paid for in some way.

'Happiness, my girl,' she said before the mirror – a cup of milky instant steaming between a photograph of her father and the enlarged coloured picture of a Labrador dog which had died four years ago – 'should be your lot, so what's all this moping for?' She wondered at herself, and took the little black Travel Aid alarm clock out of her shoulderbag and put it into a drawer of the kitchen dresser. She would be on holiday at least to that extent, by not being jangled out of sleep for the coming day, which would maybe give her dreams a chance to end naturally, and so be remembered.

two

No one could tell why George Rhoads and Bernard Missenden had never lost touch after their service in the army. Though not in any way similar, something had bound them together which took no account of their differences, each as solid in their compatibility with themselves as had been necessary to remain friends yet not really get to know each other.

All the same, forty years' acquaintance, with no quarrel either to emphasize such differences or bring them closer, must mean something, and George had wondered what it could be, in those moments of reflection which he had made sure came frequently enough to keep his life precariously on balance but which had ended his marriage. No clear answer had come to him by the time they were in the Volvo hire car being driven to London Airport. He hadn't expected it, answers being strictly reserved for the angels.

As for Bernard, he had never been able – or willing – to take time off from living even to wonder, a state that had kept him going through a second marriage and a number of affairs, for which George envied him.

High and cleanly shaped cumulus kept the weather fine. 'We can't want it better for lift-off.' Bernard was a tall saturnine Englishman, and he knew it, forever able to act the part only because that was what he was. Even his photographic stance by the remote Malayan pool as a youth of twenty had proclaimed pride in his self-awareness, suggesting that he was not dissatisfied with such an attitude, since he would get more out of life if he did not let it bother him than if he did, showing that early photographs, George thought, albeit in black and white, and maybe even for that reason, did not lie.

But Bernard's saturnine aspect was losing sharpness, hair betraying age as much as the set mouth, the scored features, flesh no longer pink and lively, and the veined back of his refined hand. When he looked in the mirror before shaving the same old handsome lines gazed back, a nonchalant wink of greeting from the left eye, but on examining recent photographs it was all he could do not to become despondent at the wear and tear.

Both were used to travelling alone, or being in charge when with more than one person, such as wife and children or, in George's case, shepherding schoolkids to Calais or beyond. Their children had children of their own, and Bernard's wife preferred, on this trip anyway, to stay behind. And now it still seemed like travelling alone, or so anybody might have thought when he and George began walking on different courses to where they supposed the checking-in point to be, until both spotted the correct place at the same moment and began to converge, two tall travellers parting the colourful mass of people who were in stasis but ready to fly apart should some malicious spirit press the button.

'Club Class.' George undid his brown sports coat, suddenly hot in his tie and shirt and fawn cardigan, slacks and socks and mirror-polished shoes.

Every other weigh desk had a tail of people, as if lining up to get holy writ from the pulpit, pushing their cases forward as barter. 'Never stood in line in my life,' Bernard said.

'We did in the army.'

'Not for long. The cooks moved us through pretty quickly.' Bernard, in his nonchalance, noticed her: light coat overarm, halfway down the queue for tourist class; a white Fair Isle sweater, an eight-pointed purple brooch with a tiny silver cross in the middle just under her subtly lined throat, fair greyish hair like a halo. She looked away as he and George were called forward.

The woman at the security check emptied George's bag, nosed into everything, a stern-faced upholder of something or other, with right too plainly on her side. Maybe he would have felt better if she had been his aunt or sister. He was asked to open the whisky flask, cigar tin, rolls of film, and take the binoculars from their case. She poked into the battery compartment of his portable radio, and sent it through the screener twice.

Bernard, who waited on the other side till George was allowed through, surely didn't look less suspicious, in his pale blue Rohan trousers, open Jaeger shirt, Reebok shoes, and jacket overarm. 'She had your number.'

'The bloody old dragon.'

'Still, it's for our own good.'

The only reason that kept him unruffled. 'I know.'

'You should have told her how we fought the terrorists in Malaya, all those years ago.'

'Before she was born,' George said.

'Almost before we were born. But we did.'

At the tawdry glitter of the Duty Free, Bernard said: 'I don't think I'll bother. You save a pound or two, but who cares?' I sometimes feel a fool, he thought, rushing in among all the goodies with the mob.

George lit a thin cigar, not having smoked in the Volvo. Gladys had drawn the line at smoking, at least when she was in the car. You couldn't smoke in the cinema or the theatre or in the Tube any more. At home he'd had his own room to puff in. But he and Gladys had just divorced, so he did what he liked in his furnished room in Twickenham. Among the shelves and packed showcases of booze and tobacco and chocolate he tried to imagine what his long-dead father would have thought about the temptations of such a place – no feat, because Leonard Rhoads had been a part-time Methodist preacher of the West Riding, by trade an austere shopkeeper who had sent his sons via the scholarship system into grammar school and on to University. A non-smoking teetotaller, as well as a pacifist, he had all but said the service of the dead over George when he volunteered for the army at seventeen. Even though the War had ended, and he was only sent to Malaya, and he would have been called up a few months later anyway, he could hardly forgive him, a rigidity which would have seared the mother's heart had the old man not relented (George smiled: he was nearly twenty years younger than I am now) and accepted him in the style of the Prodigal when he came back from the East. But George went south after University, and saw his father barely half a dozen times before he died. No, the old man certainly wouldn't be seen in a place like this, may he rest in peace. 'We're going to a Moslem country,' he said, 'and booze might be scarce, or dear. It wouldn't harm us to get a bottle of Scotch each.'

'You're right, by God.' Bernard observed the girl at the cash desk, with upstanding blond hair, grey eyes bordered with shadow, turned up nose, face dulled with leaden make-up, striped shirt to de-emphasize a heavy bosom.

'You're staring a bit, aren't you?' George said.

'She looked at me.'

'So what?'

'I think she's fallen in love with me.'

George took his arm. 'Come on, she's not for a broken down old bastard like you.'

'You cheeky devil!'

'Nor me, more's the pity.'

But Bernard knew better. 'We're experienced, we're fatherly (and a lot of 'em like that), not unhandsome – speaking for myself – and we've got a pound or two which we aren't shy of spending.'

'One way of putting it,' George said.

'The only way. What a shame we can't live forever. I'm just beginning to enjoy life. Every year that goes by I feel I'm getting too old to die!'

They laughed, and walked through the turnstile, divided by shelves of booze and tobacco.

Travelling Club Class, they were let into the Courtesy Lounge. 'Free drinks.' Bernard returned from the bar with a plate of peanuts and a double Scotch. George had coffee, glancing around as he stirred: two score people, nearly all men. 'We were lucky to find a seat,' Bernard said. 'Even the mob goes Club these days. Still, not a bad place to pass an hour. They're looking after us.' His hand went among the peanuts. 'Travellers Anonymous – a great organization.' He downed the Scotch and went for another.

'Keep an eye on Bernard,' Jenny had said. 'Don't let him get too drunk, or catch you-know-what' – half serious, George supposed, because no one could be his brother's keeper these days, at the age they were, and both long settled in the ways of the world. Open and generous beyond whatever the norm might be, Jenny had telephoned eighteen months ago. 'I'm planning Bernard's sixtieth birthday treat.'

'It's a bit soon, isn't it?'

She laughed. 'Well, it is, but you're going to be in on it.'

'Don't be funny.'

'I'm buying him a trip to Malaya. He's talked about it ever since I've known him. So it would be nice if he went back.'

'You might be right,' he said cautiously.

'And he can't go alone.'

'He's a big boy.'

'And how! But wouldn't it be nice for him to have one of his old friends to go with him? Two chaps together, eh?'

'You mean me?'

'Will you be available?'

'I'm retiring next year. Free as the wind.'

'That's all right, then. I pay for you as well. But don't tell him, that's all I ask. It's got to be a secret till about a week before you go.'

He saw it as one of those ideas that come and go in the night, but Jenny planned it to the last jot and tittle, and with such cunning that no wonder Bernard couldn't believe it when she handed him the tickets.

Bernard was quite capable of seeing to himself, being an international bookdealer, salesman manager of the publishing world, but Jenny enlisted George's support because Bernard might not have wanted to go on his own, could have balked at the last minute, seen it as a waste of time, possibly of expense, as well as being wary of tampering with a vital ghost of his past. Bernard returned with two more doubles. 'Cheers!'

'Cheers, then! A few drinks to fuzz the shock, as much as settle the thirst.'

'We're on the move,' Bernard said. 'I can hardly believe it.'

'Nor me. Malaya, of all places.'

'You've got to be joking.'

'I'm happy I'm not.'

'Let's drink to it.' A few businessmen, briefcases by their suede shoes, wondered why the ceremonial tapping of glasses. 'Cheers!'

Besides hand luggage they kept plastic bags of duty free close to their knees. Such caution would, Bernard thought, be a dummy run for Malaya, because a guidebook for backpackers said that thieving was prevalent, advised money belts and case locks. Overcare was bad for the calm mind, but as it had been normal all his life, with one or two unfortunate exceptions, he would rely on the zipped up front pocket of his trousers to keep cheques and passport safe from magnetized fingers. He held his drink high, as if to see a topless bather through the blur. 'We're so early we'll probably miss the plane.'

Jenny wouldn't like that, after her clandestine planning. 'We'll hear it over the tannoy in good time, I should think,' George said.

'So we will. Cheers!'

'Cheers! Do you want another?'

'I do. But I shan't.'

'Nor me. I must have a slash, though.' George made his way over stretched legs, wondering how it could be that he was dropping so soon into the old lingo. Following the signs to the bog – you see? – he knew that Jenny might not indeed relish it should anything stop them getting airborne. He had picked up her horror at such a notion, as if she thought Bernard's subconscious would manufacture some last minute turmoil that would land him – or them – back at the door, in revenge for the subterfuge he had never suspected in her, and which at first, mingled with gratitude, had set up a faint timbrel of alarm in him. But in the car ride to Heathrow Bernard had expressed his love and appreciative wonder that she had set up such a unique birthday gift. 'I do hope all goes well,' she said in the bedroom while he was putting things into his case. George had gone up from London to stay a preliminary couple of days at their Buckinghamshire house, a place complete with stable and paddock, swimming pool and tennis court, left to Bernard by his old man who had made a killing as a barrister.

'Take care,' she said to Bernard. 'And when you get back, look for a welcoming note in the message rack' – no fine detail omitted from their travel package. A woman like that would have been a great asset in the War. George had known her for donkey's years, yet they had met only half a dozen times. She was an all-gung-ho-chaps type, yet nice natured, though George felt a tension, almost a worry in her close-set eyes which Bernard most likely, as is often the case with husbands, couldn't see. Nothing to fear at them going off like angels on such a trip, which she had brought about, after all, though George knew he wasn't mistaken in her hope that he hadn't detected her mood of anxiety. It may have been perfectly normal for a wife to worry, but it wasn't for Jenny.

A cracked voice from the speaker behind his head, as if the wardress type of woman was banging her fist on a walnut between each syllable, indicated, much against her wishes, that their flight could proceed to the boarding gate. He zipped up too quickly, drops all over the place, hoping Bernard hadn't wandered, never to be seen again.

George opened the door. Couldn't care less. Never had cared less, about him or anybody. Well, no, not true, must speak the truth – even to himself. He deserved as much, had cared to the extent that he had lost all his ginger thatch by thirty, sported a dental plate by forty, had a bit of a break-down by leaving his wife at fifty (but he'd gone back three weeks later), been divorced by sixty – though right now he felt more like himself than he ever had, a shame to have waited so long.

Bernard stood with bags hoisted, looking around, as if wondering who, in his right mind, would go on such a trip. Yet he couldn't remember when he had been so excited, though to look at his all-cognizant expression as he moved towards the door no one would know. 'Come on, let's feed ourselves into the canning mill.'

Drenched in light, the Boeing waited for its four hundred passengers, meanwhile replenished with food and drink by a litter of supply trucks, and suckled by a bowser-queue pumping a hundred and forty tons of prime octane into the tanks to ensure lift-off. 'You'd get a row of old Dakotas on its wings.' In the final departure hall Bernard recalled their flight in one up the coast of Malaya after the Emergency began – pinned with kit along the aluminium floorboards, grey traces of cloud occasionally darkening a window by George's head.

'A bumpy old banger, reeking with petrol and peardrops.' George looked over his shoulder at the magazine. 'What lovely breasts she has. Still, I wouldn't like to drop a match among all that petrol.'

You go through the most intense light to get to the dark, and through the most incinerating heat to reach the cold – and stay there forever. Such an experience wouldn't appeal to Bernard, though the flash registered in his brown-grey eyes. 'I'd like to see it, but not be in it. From afar, that is to say, through a pair of good binoculars. In the meantime, don't look too obviously, but take a glance at that woman standing rather offish over there, at about three of the clock. I registered her at the checking-in desk. What mystery and promise in the tilt of her otherwise plain features. She's not going Club Class, I regret to say, more's the pity.' He waved, as if to go over and talk, but dropped his magazine and had to pick it up because the announcement came for them to move. George noticed her smile, but whether at him, or Bernard, or at some recollected antics of The Three Stooges, he couldn't say.

Boarding cards in hand, they clomped along the plastic tunnel towards the doors of the plane, where a smiling brown-skinned woman in the sober colours of the East looked at their seat numbers. 'I'm in love with her already.' George paused on the spiral staircase leading to the penthouse deck.

'Too young for you,' Bernard said. 'The perfect age for a man's mistress, according to the French, as I must have read somewhere (and the French always have a word for it, bless 'em) is half his age plus seven, which means also that you change her every year. Still, I suppose any man can be forgiven for coveting these fresh young things. A matter of making the right choice, though.'

And for a woman who wants a lover, George supposed she'd choose one who was half her age *minus* seven, but he didn't mention this to Bernard. At half past nine, no sign of take-off, a whisky was served, bedsocks brought, and rolled face flannels handed out with tweezers like hot pancakes for eating. 'Soft music on the Kipling Express,' Bernard chimed. 'I still can't get over it. Beyond the blue horizon, and China across the Bay. Club Class to Raffles!' His soul ached from the separation, always the same anguish at being away from home. A trip on his own was looked forward to as a skive, work or no work, bliss to be at the mercy of chance meetings in strange places, but as soon as it happened he was bereft, wondered where the hell he was and why the hell he had allowed it to come about, knowing from previous times that three days must go by before the torment abated – meanwhile hiding his perturbations from George, his oldest friend who was nevertheless a stranger.

The windows were beaded with rain. 'The goodbye kiss of Blighty. When the troopship left Southampton in 1946,' George said, 'we went down the Solent in bright sunshine.'

The captain announced that they were awaiting a slot in the departure arrangements. 'I left from Liverpool,' Bernard recalled, 'and everybody on the old tub sicked up the whole way to Gibraltar. Going through the Med I had six jabs for all the heathen diseases we might encounter. I woke one morning to look through the porthole from my hammock, and what did I see?'

'A bloke riding a camel along the banks of the Suez Canal.'

'I was amazed.' Maybe neither of us have yet recovered from the shock. 'We were lucky lads.' Bernard's smile was the puzzled expression of a sixty-year-old – lined face, shuttered mouth, eyes that could no longer be surprised – imposed on the supercilious fire of a youth who even in those far-off days had decided to live forever. 'And now we're going back.'

They clinked glasses – no plastic beakers in Club Class. 'It must be the most original birthday present of the century,' George said. 'We'll have a lot to tell Jenny.'

At half-ten local time the plane trundled towards the runway, airport lights like candles in tins. Bloody grim out there, England under the eternal wash of benign rain. Bernard didn't like it. Yet sweet air had come into the living room while he was packing, Jenny in the doorway, hands uncharacteristically over her bosom. She was fifty but looked scarcely forty, tall, fair, clear skinned, full of salty humour, a well contained figure, yummy to any strange man, he had noticed, whenever they walked into a restaurant. But in a recent hot argument he had called out that she was a bloody old woman, to which she replied that she felt it, living with a crumbling old cantankerous bastard like him. Oh those wicked fights, they never stopped, each giving as good as they got, and worse – or better, depending on whether or not the mudpies stuck. As for him, if he lived to be a hundred he would never acknowledge feeling old, not to anyone, not even when he admitted it to himself. Such dark moments were invariably padded with humour, disbelief, and even scorn, so that little harm came of them. Why run yourself down when you had an obliging wife to do it for you?

Their set-to had brewed up after his secretary Helen had, to assuage an attack of guilt, confessed to Jenny about one of their delectable romps together. Jenny was a onetime school friend of Helen's mother, and Helen must have heard them talking about old friendships, trust and love – and blown the gaff. How was he to know she was neurotic as well as sexy? She had the most wonderful tits, often the case with someone who couldn't be trusted. Five years ago he had been to bed with Helen's mother, a secrecy pact never broken, proving that the young ones were far more mixed up than ever the old ones used to be, the only pity being that the old ones got too old and had to be gently put aside.

But anyway, funny or not, there was Jenny in the doorway, and in recompense for the grind she had put him through for his misdemeanour (thank God she hadn't found out about a few other near misses) had engineered this birthday present of sending him to Malaya. 'I can't believe it,' he said. 'Going back to the place after all these years.'

'I hope you enjoy it.'

'Oh, I'm sure I shall. But what a tremendous idea.'

She kissed him. 'It's the least I can do.'

'I feel awful, leaving you for two weeks.'

'Just bring back some nice presents.'

His case was a jumble, but he pressed it shut, unsure of the expedition, couldn't understand it. Her hand trembled in straightening his jacket. 'I wanted to get a really unforgettable present for your sixtieth.'

She had always taken care over such matters, her consideration in the family famous, but with this one he was tempted to regret every affair he'd had, or the ones she had found out about, though he saw no reason to regret what had been so natural and, let's face it, pleasant. He loved her, all the same, gratified that he had never ceased to tell her so. 'You're marvellous. I'll always love you.'

Tell even the most hardened woman that you love her, croon away with sufficient conviction, and sooner or later she will give in to you, providing of course (naturally) that you are likeable. In any case he couldn't say such a thing without being deeply sincere, you had to be, as he knew that he would have been impressed if a woman had said she was in love with him, though such cases had been very scattered along the horizon. The only woman who ever had said it as if she had meant it was Jenny, and he had married her.

Burning turbofans pushed the four hundred residential tons through cloud and into the uptilted basin of stars, levelled off at thirty-odd thousand feet, and got into its stride of near six hundred miles an hour. At such moments George felt he was leaving England never to return, but then, he always had, even when he used to take his schoolkids on day trips to Calais, and the boat slid from the grey embrace of Dover. The menu for dinner was produced. 'A promising speed to the service.'

Bernard grimaced, after a prolonged scrutiny of the typing. 'A disappointment, though, not to get Malayan food.'

'Malaysian, these days.'

'I was in Malaya, so Malaya it will always be.'

'They might get offended,' George said, 'if we use the old colonial name.'

He fanned himself with the menu. 'They wouldn't have any name at all if we hadn't saved them from the horrors of communist misery. I hope they appreciate how we suffered.'

'Sweating over Lion Lager in the NAAFI,' George said. 'Having to share a servant with four others. Three-course meals in the mess. Our own beach to swim from, a sailing boat to play around with, holiday leave on Muong Island, nobody to bother us as long as we went out on patrol now and again. What a hard time we had! A coconut fell from a tree once, and nearly killed me.'

Bernard laughed. 'Slogging through the jungle for six bob a day. The poor bloody infantry, that's what we were.'

Whatever the truth, and hard to know from so long afterwards, the stewardesses must think we're a right pair. 'Roast loin of veal for me,' George said. 'Buttered turnips, sautéed french beans, buttered tagliatelle. Can't be bad.'

'I'll have the Aylesbury duck.' Bernard peered through his bifocal contact lenses. 'Plus the trimmings. Couldn't live without the trimmings. My girlfriend says she gets more pleasure out of the trimmings these days than the real thing. A damned cheek, but she may be right. Nice *hors d'oeuvres*, I see, though it's a disappointment not to get *nasi goreng* with an egg on top. Remember? A Third World country ashamed of its classical grub and trying to palm us off with pseudo-French is nothing short of effrontery.' He looked ahead, a shimmer of disturbance, as if he really might be upset enough to bother the stewardess. She smiled, her lovely bosom towards them, alas too well clothed, and handed them a card which unfortunately, Bernard thought, won't have her private telephone number on it. 'To fill in, before arrival at Singapore.'

'Thank you so much.' He pulled a slim Mont Blanc from

his travelling bag. 'No such thing as embarkation cards last time we went. Filed off the troopship with a kitbag and rifle. They just like to keep us busy, I suppose.'

Capital letters blazed out in red: DEATH TO DRUG TRAFFICKERS. 'Too late to chuck our dope overboard,' George said. 'Good yarn it would make if Jenny had thought to buy you a suitcase with a fake bottom and stuffed it with a few ounces of cocaine. Are you sure she didn't buy you a new one for the occasion? Gladys would, if we hadn't been divorced. She'd have said the old one was too battered for such a pregnant trip.'

Bernard dropped his passport, had to feel under the seat. 'I wish you would choke on your gallows humour.'

'Hard not to think what a right pair we'd look dangling from the gibbet. The successful conclusion to a well organized plot. Women's Lib strikes again!'

Such ingenuity, Bernard decided, was beyond the wiles of his wife, fiendishness not part of her nature. And yet, if Jenny had thought of it would she have done it? He sweated, had loved her too much ever to have felt malice towards her, proved by the fact that he had always kept his affairs as secret as was humanly possible. Even when she had gone inside a few days to have a melanomic scab taken from the small of her back he had devised alibis for every hour of her absence, and if she hadn't quite believed him she must have appreciated the skill of the storyteller. He jabbed George in the ribs. 'You're round the bend and halfway up the zigzags. You always were, especially in the old days.'

'That made two of us, the craziest bastards in the platoon. And look at us now. We were young and crazy, now we're old and crazy. I suppose it's no bad thing they take this drug business seriously. Laws like that must cut it down a bit.'

'I can't disagree, either.'

George's son had been silly on them from sixteen up, became a registered drug addict fed an allowance by the state. One Monday morning, ten years later, he didn't sign on for his drugs. Didn't want them any more. He'd fallen in love, so got a job, saw a house he liked, married when his girlfriend got pregnant, as happy as anybody could be. But what chemical permutation of the soul or the physical body had set him to making that first decision to lay off the filth? Or to begin it, for that matter? George had wanted to ask, but didn't care to upset the subtle balance re-established between himself and his son, and later it wasn't important. 'Well, you can't hang someone for smoking pot. Don't think I would hang anyone for anything, for that matter.'

'I would,' Bernard said. 'Muggers, for instance, who rape. Terrorists, I'd shoot to kill, just like terrorists themselves do. Like we did, in the jungle. An eye for an eye. I can't help but believe in it.'

'Youngsters don't feel like that.'

'I'll bet plenty of them do. And those who don't will when they get older and see sense. Still, can't say I feel very bloodthirsty with these lovely little hostesses going up and down the gangway.' Half an hour since take-off, two glasses of red wine were put under their noses. 'Thick and heavy.' He tasted it. 'But indisputably wine.'

'Plonk.' George had a swig. 'Algeria's revenge. Here's to the hole in your stomach.'

'Rubber legs.'

'Balsa arms.'

'Jelly arse.'

'And no fucking brains at all,' they sang.

'Cheers!'

'Cheers!'

The stewardesses passed quickly, as if on their way to the captain, who would come down the gangway on stilts and read the riot act. Fifteen minutes later they got the canapés. Bernard stabbed a roll of fat around grease circling a cold olive. 'Never a dull moment if they keep us stoked up like this.'

'Not so bad if you drink going from west to east, so I read

in a book on jet lag, but too much slurping on the return trip and it'll take weeks to re-establish our equilibrium.' He held out his glass for more wine.

A voice on the tannoy said that Munich was five miles down through the clouds. Bernard never missed his cue. 'Got your brolly, old boy?'

'It's not the monsoon season. Still' – he stood up – 'reminds me I need a leak.'

Bernard let him by. 'Didn't know it was St David's Day.'

'Stuff it, for Christ's sake.' George wondered if it was age, or because he drank more in order to ease his way through life. Rare if he didn't get up during the night. Washing hands, he saw himself, tonsure of reddish hair around a bald and mottled pate. Uneven and tobacco-stained teeth gave a piratical look when he smiled in recognition of his image flashing the first smile. Best to smile, his aspect might otherwise deceive people, himself most of all, into assuming he was trustworthy, and thus fundamentally dull. A lifetime of being a schoolteacher had convinced him that he was not, even if only because the kids had believed in him.

'I've ordered a flagon of champagne,' Bernard said. 'Which might be a better bet than the old red biddy.'

George unfolded *The Times*, and looked at the first tormenting clue of the crossword, which he hoped to finish by the fortnight's end. 'If I had worked at the Foreign Office I suppose I'd do it before my egg boiled.'

'Not the one in *Pravda*?' Bernard considered the champagne to be stony, vinegar-tasting stuff, the first mouthful fizzling in his throat. He turned to spray it loose, but let it gently descend when the eversmiling girl came to spread linen cloths over their tables. 'What a bevy of pretty malkins! Lovely to think we've still got thirteen hours to go.' The first course was crab, with more champagne. 'The second glass always tastes better, no matter how bad it is,' he said, the bon viveur of the publishing world.

Veal and red wine were followed by fruit, cheese and trifle.

George balked at the brandy. 'Burns my stomach all night, and I have a critical hangover in the morning.' By clearing up time the old troopship would have been ten days at sea to get to the same place.

'Three hours we've been up. I suppose you're just right. Amazing.' Bernard yawned. What a hole in life my life makes. Three hours lost, but then so much is. Life was full of holes he would have fallen through if he hadn't continually won the fight to block them up. Pour delicious food into them so as to decoy any black dogs that might come running through. Placard them with exquisite *trompe-l'oeils* of travel scenes. Let the Devils slip and break their limbs on the life-giving fluid pumped into wife and girlfriends as often as he was capable – as they came hot-scenting through a hole to tear his equilibrium to pieces. Baffle the black holes before they turned into mouths.

'For me,' George said, 'the Med was stormy from Gib to Port Said. I had a tooth out, as well as the jabs, which stopped me being seasick when everybody else was.'

Bernard made a gargoyle face. 'I swear this coffee's decaffeinated.'

'It's too weak to know. They want us to sleep, I suppose.'

'Probably laced with bromide. Keep us impotent for the next fortnight.'

'I've been impotent for a decade, so it won't make any difference.'

'Really?'

George, ironic from birth, was by no means sure that Bernard had picked up his tone. No matter. Whether they had any temperament to share or not it was only for fourteen days, the length of a leave, and they would no doubt revel more sincerely in each other's company when they clapped eyes on the old place. For in the beginning – after the word – was friendship, and the end of friendship – as of the word – would be nothing more than blackness, especially between him and Bernard, because on one memorable patrol in the jungle Bernard didn't blast off like an automaton with his Short Lee-Enfield when the shooting started but first pushed George into the vegetable mud, George swearing hot cinders till Bernard got up and they fired like the rest but from better cover at the bandits trying to break out of the forest so as to terrorize innocent people into giving them support. Chaos accounted for everything, but the weird matter to George was that he himself hadn't thought of protecting anyone, certainly not Bernard, the only other person in the platoon as barmy as he had felt himself to be from birth, and whose instinct had led him to act for others before himself. Thereafter they talked about the ambush, bullets stone-chatting into the trees, as nothing more than a confused occurrence at the end of a long search.

They were going back – on a nostalgia tour to find out whether or not those faded black and white photographs stuck in the disintegrating sellotaped albums had any meaning. Bernard never mentioned the incident in the jungle, but George knew that no one ever forgot, there being more to Bernard than one would normally assume in a mere executive salesman. The memory of such qualities could never be deracinated, because the past was a buried container of coal mulch coated with the plant life of the present, which had changed from the jungle they had been in to the shallower clay of existence since. George, surprised at the intensity of his feelings, drifted into sleep that no hooks could dig into and disturb.

Bernard couldn't even doze, watched the B movie. On a troopship you settled down and knew it was forever, the smoke-stacked snail sliming a great circle along the wet belly of the world, but on a plane the oncoming minute was always a possible end, the plane disintegrating, bits and bodies spinning to earth, after a bomb had punctured the precious envelope. The minute that came after brought the gnawing pain of boredom, and the minute after the minute of hope that followed would have been unendurable if another minute of hope hadn't immediately replaced it. That was life, every minute exciting, the skin eternally pricked with optimism and disappointment. But despair? Never. Despair is the curse of those who labour with the soul, and he thanked God he wasn't one of those, unlike poor old George, who had taken his career as a teacher solemnly indeed, but whom he nevertheless envied for sleeping peacefully on the uptilted seat by his side.

The monster plane droned with a consistent tone that held them in a cocoon of silence. In that sense life was silent, till a disturbance reminded you that you had better not think so. Bernard's life was as much battered with turbulence when he was on the ground as George's these days seemed filled with silence. But the silence they now shared was more George's than his. Being unaccustomed to silence, he couldn't sleep. And being used to silence, George could, though Bernard did not envy him, merely thought him lucky because he had something that he had not, though in normal times he considered himself the luckier of the two, cock of the roistering walk – George's life a dull toothache compared to Bernard's hole in the head.

He didn't know he was asleep till he was awakened at half past seven by George fiddling with the map, ruler and a page of figures. 'By dead reckoning we must have crossed the coast of India.'

'I suppose you're waiting for the pilot to come up and say: "I've got to be frank, George. I'm lost. We slept too long up front. The inertial navigation system's on the blink, and the radio's dead. Can't hear a single beacon, and I've forgotten how to work the sextant for a how-do-ye-do. So where are we?" Then you can show him the map and put him right. He then asks you, of course, to work the co-pilot's stint – who went down with salmonella from eating our leftovers – and we get a heroes' welcome at Changi, made honorary crew members with free travel for the rest of our lives.'

George cheered. 'And we'll be twenty years old again, with never a thought about the future in our little adolescent brains.'

'My mouth's like a gorilla's shithouse after the Last Supper.' Bernard slumped back, a twist of the lips. 'If you'll forgive the blasphemous expression. Which only a sustained bout of breakfast will cure. When I miss out on sleep I feel I've drunk too much, and when I've drunk too much I feel I've had no sleep. Now it's a bit of both and I don't know where I am.'

George gazed out of the window. 'Nothing but ocean. There are stratus clouds a bit below us, though.' Half past nine in the morning, British Summer Time. Land – the southern islands of the Andaman Group – with the paradise of Car Nicobar to the north. 'Two hours before Singapore, and I hear the pleasing rattle of cutlery. Do you remember when the RAF sent Lincoln bombers from Ceylon to help us douse the terrorists? They blew up a lot of jungle, those Brylcreem Boys.'

Bernard yawned. 'What a wonderful time we had.'

George wondered how much of the old place had changed.

'Not as much as we have, I'm sure.'

The girl had a lively smile, as if she had slept the sleep of the young and the good. Orange juice, coffee, a bowl of cornflakes with fresh milk, a basket of fruit and a hot croissant: hard to know where to start, or how. Bernard tore a blue-black grape from its stem. 'The cabin crew's been changed while the plane kept flying. Being the best airline in the world they arrange for two jumbos to fly side by side, with connecting chutes for stewardesses to shoot along and change shifts. Who figured out such a system, I wonder?'

Coffee swept a sunken lane through George's gullet. 'A British invention, no doubt.'

Stage two for Bernard was bacon, mushrooms, and a breadroll. 'I'm more in love with her than ever.'

'Which one?'

'How should I know? They're all so exquisite that they look the same. I wouldn't mind one. Two would be even better.' He tried to see them naked but they were somehow too real, too close, too slick and manicured – never close enough, like the half-clothed girls at the old Windmill Theatre which his father had taken him to on his fourteenth birthday, the only move towards letting him know the so-called facts of life. 'We're going out on a treat tonight, you and I, young Bernard, my lad.' A front seat, and through the cigar smoke those personable women still weren't close enough, and his father laughed when he put out an arm as if to touch. Halfway through the show the sirens went, and left an excitement he never forgot, of half-naked women and the clatter of artillery as they ran to the Tube station.

George spaded into a Mexican omelette. 'I saw you trying to feel her up. The captain will make you walk the plank. Thirty-five thousand feet is a long way to fall.' A fourteen-hour suspension in the never-never land of a Jumbo was better than the one George had taken off from, a land in which he had never felt as free as now, going to a grainy black and white far-off photo-land of the past, a place where he hadn't been free either but in which companionship and the obligation of duty had made a paradise for the soul. That, of course, was in retrospect, the reality of those two years distorted by the lapsing of time, a memory soon to be brutalized, he shouldn't wonder, by the error of going back and stamping on that idealized dream once and for all.

'I still can't get over it,' Bernard said, two hours before landing. 'To be seeing the old place after forty years.'

Needless to remind him, but one pleasing revelation of the trip on George was that he could again rattle out the small talk, a facility he thought had gone forever after his divorce. The encapsulated plane journey brought back sensible elation.

He scratched words into his notebook, wanting to keep a full account of such a trip, till the stewardess came with a tray of pens in leather cases, free souvenirs of the airline. 'No excuse for not writing postcards, either,' Bernard said. 'All my girlfriends expect one. A dozen to the lovely wife, of course. Life's all go. My ex-girlfriends, as well. One of them had the best tits I've ever come across. I'll send her two. They're probably no good now, after having had four kids.'

George wondered how the pen was held together. 'You're too generous.'

'Never hurt anyone. When I meet her in the street I tell her I love her still. Nothing wrong in making them happy. Brings tears of gratitude to her eyes. It's always true, when I say it. I like to make all women happy. They deserve it, poor souls.'

The pen flew apart, scattering the top, two screws, the main body, the ink spine. 'I should have left well alone,' George said. Everything he had ever touched had sprayed asunder, uncontrollable, impossible to put back in place. His heart bumped while getting bits from under the seat, crimson-faced as he fitted the pieces together, a late-in-life achievement for his unmechanical soul.

Outside there was blue sky and sea, cloud to the north, Sumatra forming the starboard smudge-line. He calculated that at ten-forty they would see Malaya, but land came a few minutes earlier, the flat coast cut at a sharper angle, grey rivers convoluting through mangrove swamps. The petrolometers of a port were pillboxes clustered at the edge of the water. 'Probably Port Swettenham, but they call it Pelabuhan these days. Hard for us old hands to use a name like that.'

'Why the hell should we?' Bernard grumbled.

'I couldn't agree more.' Sombre cumulus hung over the backbone of mountains, hard to distinguish true relief from such a height. A tremor of excitement lay in him somewhere, overscored by fatigue after twelve hours airborne.

Bernard leaned across. 'Not much to see,' opened his notebook, looked at his watch, and borrowed the map to record matters. George wondered how their notes differed, both assiduously writing, quick to get it over. Probably thinking I'm a bit cool for showing so little enthusiasm after Jenny troubled to get us up here. All in all he wondered whether they hadn't left it too late, should have come only ten or a dozen years after the event except that, funnily enough, he hadn't been interested, hardly thought of the place, and now such long absence had squeezed all excitement out.

Thick-packed cloud over the mountains turned as white as snow, an Antarctic landscape of Yetis and Pushpakkas, those ancient Indian flying machines hidden behind each peak. A cosmic shower of spray lay static above one bulbous summit, a white but warty hill frozen in mid-explosion. Tuber roots and grotesque dolls' heads made a gigantic sculpture gallery in snow. 'It's seven in the evening, local time,' George said. 'We've lost a whole day. I suppose we'd better change our watches, or we won't know when it's time for supper.'

Bernard agreed. 'We look set for a bumpy descent through all that fluff.'

three

Straight wide boulevards flanked by plants and trees, massive blocks of flats beyond, all neat, pink-white and light brown, drawing them into the centre of the conurbation. They were silent, and darkness happened from the taxi turning off one freeway to settling onto another, lights by the million reflecting against low cloud covering the island.

Under the arcade of the Dragon Hotel a uniformed janissary of the Sultan's guard opened the door, and an apprentice bellhop boy-soldier trollied their cases to the signing-in desk. 'Good to travel in style.'

'It's best never to do anything else,' Bernard said. 'We might be dead next week.'

George found the hotel characterless, one of the so-called luxury sort newly put up all over the world in the last decade or so, a jumped-up All-Bernie place.

'The old-fashioned hotels must also have been built at the same time,' Bernard said, 'and were no doubt considered brash compared to the pigsties and pot houses they had replaced.'

Certainly, the womb comfort could not be gainsaid. Exquisite politeness from beautiful women, a mere form to fill in, and you had only to walk to the lift, and at a room on the twenty-fourth floor find the boy-soldier already setting down your cases, for which George settled on him the equivalent of a pound.

'Chucking your akkers around, aren't you?'

'Poor buggers have to live.'

'Sentiment,' Bernard said. 'We paid our bearer a dollar a week, if I'm not mistaken.'

George tried to put on more lights but no switch responded. 'Either we hot-wire the candlepower, or phone the desk to say we can't figure out the system. If the lights aren't brighter than this we won't be able to read.'

Bernard went around plicking buttons. 'Must be a master switch somewhere.'

Nothing behind the curtains, under the beds, tacked on the walls. Everything was flush and built-in. George took a whisky flask from his bag. 'Any glasses in the bathroom?'

'Nothing like a drop of the golden fluid to give us inspiration. Cheers!'

'Cheers!'

Bernard ambled to a contraption by the door, slotted in the credit card type keyholder, and all lights came on. 'The cunning devils – just to stop you going out without putting the glow worms back in their box.'

Beyond the window a million volts made a beautiful waste of lights over the city. 'Don't see the sense of it,' George said.

'I expect the Japs sold 'em a pup. They sold us a few, too. Very good at selling pups, the Japs.'

'Bit racist, aren't you?'

'Not more than they are, I expect.'

'Still, you figured out their lighting system.'

'It's just that there's a difference between them and us, and it doesn't harm them, or us, to recognize it.'

George mulled on his definition of racism, didn't make much of it, so tilted his leather flask over the glass. 'Another splash?'

'You shave first. Only don't take too long. I'm famished.'

Changed into smart khaki and white sneakers, Bernard stood in the bathroom doorway while George safety-razored soap and stubble from his jutting chin. 'A friend at the firm told me about an area of Chinese cookshops called Woolsthorpe Circle. We can ask about it at the desk.'

The taxi driver was a grey bearded Sikh, from whose radio came a loud metrical iteration of prayer throughout the (thank God) shortish trip. Bernard wanted to strangle the old bastard for foisting his religious service on them in such an obviously aggressive way, and gave him no tip, but since tips weren't *de rigueur* in Singapore anyway the old bastard hadn't noticed his displeasure, and might have been more happy if he had. Getting into a taxi in these parts was like being invited into somebody's house, though they hardly treated you as an honoured guest, with requests not to smoke spit or fornicate, and jungle music pestling your brain to mush.

Food smells enlivened them, lights searing at the cook stalls, and plenty of people crowding tables or standing to make their choices, or watching raw materials shaken into steaming vats. 'Hard to know where to begin.'

George wore a dark blue seersucker suit culled from an Oxfam shop years ago, and a straw Panama bought back from a trip to Spain. 'Let's start with a drink, then we can look around at our leisure.'

Litre bottles of Lion Lager were served from a stack in front of a stall. 'There's no doubt about it,' Bernard said, 'those who live the easiest lives live longest.'

Glasses slopped at the brim. 'Happy days!'

'Who would have thought we would be putting back the old Lion Lager forty years later?'

George held the rim of his hat as if it might blow away. 'In those days a year seemed a lifetime. Our imagination couldn't take it in. It happened, and was gone. We were too young to have any sense of time.'

'No sense at all,' Bernard said, 'if you ask me, or we wouldn't be here now. Thinking of tomorrow would have done for us. Bashing after terrorists through the jungle, it was only the next second we were interested in, much to their discomfort, and our survival.'

'I didn't even think, in those days,' George said. 'At least I don't remember thinking. My thought processes hadn't developed.'

Bernard laughed. 'I still don't think mine have. All I've got is a stomach, a you-know-what, and an unthinking ability to do my work.'

'British to the core. Cheers!'

'Cheers! Mind you, I get to work by seven, and steal a march on the rush hour. Sometimes don't get home till nine in the evening. The trouble is that when others stop work you often have to as well.'

George didn't know what to believe. The 'often' and the 'sometimes' shaded Bernard's claims into ambiguity. He tested the extremity of his Toryism. 'Maybe we should shoot a few of the idlers.'

'Oh no! Not English idlers, bless 'em. Shoot one, and the rest would take to the hills. That sort of thing wouldn't even work with the Russians these days. Knock it back, tosh. We're too old to die young.' He stood up when all bottles were empty. 'Let's perambulate.'

They were familiar with chopsticks, though George felt less than adept when the Hokkien noodles kept slipping through. But the lifted bowl, and a more rapid delivery, soon emptied the dish.

They shared a fish, more Lion to swim in it, and two bowls of rice to bog it down. A young girl served while the mother cooked. Rounded lips, smoky eyes, full cheeks and short black hair, she observed them when their gaze was down, as if from some distant country of her own, hardly moving her head. George caught her glance, pleased at her interest, puzzled by her subtlety. Clever and intelligent, she worked hard at school, would no doubt get to university, meantime helped her mother run the cookstall and keep the home going. He would leave a few extra dollars when they paid.

Bernard beckoned for more beer. 'The same smells as forty years ago.'

'Makes you wonder where all the time's gone.'

'Doesn't interest me any more. The only question is: how much more is there to come?'

A lot, George hoped, puzzled as to how they had got onto such a sombre topic. Bernard, discarding extrovert hilarity, occasionally launched them into such moods, though he was adept at throwing them off.

'Smells never change.' Beyond the cooking zone, Singapore had lost its soul, George thought, not the same place as in the old days. Couldn't quite put his finger on it.

'Sold out to Mammon?' Bernard suggested. 'Hardly. And what if they have? They're all busy, healthy, and making money. It can't be bad, soul or no soul.'

All charm gone in highrise and freeways, like every other city in the world, never again to be the same. The revolution of utter change had squashed the old Singapore forever. He was surprised at himself.

'I agree,' Bernard said, 'but at least you can still get superb food. Anyway, the soul is inside people, not in buildings, and the soul is always better for being well fed. Remember the poor sods pulling rickshaws in the old days? Fighting for custom? Scrabbling to earn a bob or two before dying of TB? Where's the soul in that?'

They waited twenty minutes, and still no vacant taxi, so George navigated them down the wide boulevard between blocks of flats, monsoon ditches six feet deep. 'Must rain a bucket when it does.'

'As we well remember,' Bernard said. 'How much more to go?'

He read the map from the tourist newspaper under the

glow of a high lamp. 'Down Clemenceau, turn right at Cairnhill, jink into Bideford, then we'll see the Dragon Hotel blazing with light. Less than a mile, I should think.'

Swallows flittered about the large room, hoping for spilled peanuts or shards of potato crisp.

They dropped with relief into long armchairs, after schlepping a couple of miles down the main drag from the hotel. George wiped his forehead. 'The only way to take such heat is to get as much liquid in as the stomach will hold. I was on holiday a few years ago in Israel, and got talking to a soldier near Jericho. I fear he meant water, though.'

Waitresses drifted, hardly disturbing the swallows. 'I suppose they had waiters in the old days.' Bernard stretched his legs. 'I certainly can't imagine them letting these sweet little things loose among randy sea captains. Not that *we* came here. Out of bounds to common swaddies like us. I knew the place existed, but that was about all.'

'We couldn't have afforded it.' George looked at the bill for eleven dollars. 'It was a pint in the subsidized NAAFI, or a bottle of rice spirit from the village that sent us blind for three days.'

Bernard chipped in his share. 'Remember that South African wine we bought for Christmas? A whole bloody crate. Van der Hum, I think it was.' A tourist group, men hefty and pale, women slim and young in flowered frocks, looked in at the door, then backed out as if the highest drop of the world might be immediately behind their heels. Buses unloaded them by the score in the courtyard, to see the only bit of old Singapore remaining. 'I've never been as sick as when I sank a few pints of that goddamn van der Hum stuff. Thick and sweet, if I remember. If we'd stuck to Lion Lager we'd have been just as ill, I suppose. We certainly made the palm trees grow. Shot up no end after that Christmas.'

A few men sat by their gin slings, young to late middle

age, as if pondering what was left after having achieved their life's ambition of a drink in the Long Bar at Raffles. 'I looked in my diary this morning,' George said, 'and noticed it's forty years to the day that we went up into the jungle and got those bandits.'

'You don't say?' They called for more drinks. 'Killed half a dozen, if I remember.' Bernard pictured, grainy and indistinct, the platoon dropping from the gharry at the end of the track, splashing upriver with rifles and kit, then broaching the wall of trees on either side, a pincer movement into ambush positions. A week later they came out, covered in mud, exhausted but undiminished, almost disappointed at going back into camp just when they had got used to the life. 'We did well for twenty-year-olds. I can't believe it when I see the youngsters today.'

'They'd do just as well.' George felt tolerant, at peace. 'We'd been bred to it all through the War. Seemed the only way to get out of a rut. I was disappointed when I heard they'd dropped that funny bomb on Japan.'

Bernard banged him on the shoulder. 'How could such a lunatic like you have turned into an old stick-in-the-mud schoolteacher?'

'I had to grow up, I suppose.'

'Do you remember that snake climbing a palm tree near the tents? Birds were attacking it because it was after their eggs. While it was fending them off you grabbed its tail and swung it round your head. We ran like hell.'

'I didn't hurt it. It fell on the beach and shot into the grass.'

'Then you made little wagons out of match boxes and tied a couple of shit-beetles to them with cotton. Chariot races along the duckboards!'

He had forgotten that one. But it was true, all true. What had happened? 'The world changed, not only us. I had to set an example to the kids at school. They were the roustabouts then. But I understood their high jinks, and was as tolerant as I could be.'

'Didn't do them much good, all that Sixties stuff of letting them do their own thing. It was easier for the teacher than thinking up proper lessons. Poor little devils. Arithmetic and spelling went out of the window. Not in Singapore, though.'

'And then' – George avoided the cul de sac of that stale argument – 'I got married. Life closes in. What else could I have done? Miserable as sin, to do nothing.'

'I got married as well,' Bernard said. 'But I soon got unmarried. Then I married again, the only habit worth getting into. All I wanted was a good time. Luckily, I pulled in an income to keep it going, and being an only child I felt the full blast of the old man's will when he crossed the bar.' Even so, there were lines around his mouth, set lips suggesting he'd had his miseries between the frenetic celebrations.

George's own interior scars indicated a moonscape of life-long matrimonial conflict. He married his childhood sweetheart, and so never grew up, you might say – licking his lips at the sudden revelation. Why had the primrose path turned into a maze of thorns, no goodwill remaining between the two who were caught? Parleying on any topic signalled hairpin bends into a quarrel. Self-warning signs persuaded him to keep silent so as not to cause one. But to maintain a state of buttonlips called for a feat of control which, when managed for a while, brought from her an accusation of sulking, thus ensuring a more spectacular collision when his resolution broke, the blame then equal on both sides.

Oh George, George, could it not have been avoided? No, because to keep silent before such an onslaught of scorn was to feel cleaved down the middle, one half set at war with the other, so that the dam which had been erected during the silence invariably gave way. During the last years of her misery (and his) he wondered whether such endurance wasn't his version of malice towards her (as she in one diatribe suggested) and whether she wouldn't have left him sooner if he hadn't tried at all to keep the marriage going.

In the beginning they were made for each other, which should have warned him that they were not. They directed their sufferings onto each other because they happened to be closest, but she turned even sharper needles of self-hatred onto herself, till both grew to believe that living apart was the only solution. Perhaps she never forgave him for making their life in the South. Certainly she seemed happier now that she had gone back to Wakefield and lived alone.

There were painful moments when he thought he loved her still, and lines came to mind which he first read in the barracks library forty years ago. Stricken to the soul – though as a young soldier he was as yet unfamiliar with the torments of the heart – he put them into his notebook:

> Overlive it, lower yet, be happy, wherefore
> should I care?
> I myself must mix with action, lest I wither
> in despair.

The greatest misery, he thought, is to live with someone who doesn't know why they are unhappy. But perhaps an even greater misery for Gladys was to live with someone like him, who at first didn't know when *she* was unhappy.

Not much time to make another life, but he would have to if his existence was to mean anything. When you were dead what was the meaning of meaning anyway? Such questions that had stopped him acting couldn't be allowed to affect him now. Yet if you stopped the questions you were dead even if you acted, a risk no one ought to take. 'Funny the thoughts that come to you in a place like this.'

'Mine come wherever I am, I'm afraid,' Bernard said. 'But I'm glad when they don't. Life's too short.' He stood, and braced himself. 'I feel like wrecking the place.'

George was tired of such irritating looniness, including his own. They were different people when alone, would be unrecognizable now to their various acquaintances. He was not himself when with Bernard, no more than Bernard was himself when with him, or so he assumed. Strange how the human chemistry varied according to who you were with. Being with Bernard made him want to be on his own, in the hope of getting back to who he really was. Yet if he did, the effect might be so neutral that he wouldn't be able to recognize himself. Nor, which was worse, would anyone else know how to place him, for he knew he was not so naïve as to imagine that such rules applied to anyone but himself. 'Another time.'

Bernard sat down, unclenched his fists, and called a waitress.

'Yes, sir?'

'My friend here has just divorced his wife, and he would like to marry you.'

Skin puckered at the bridge of her nose.

'Two more beers,' George said.

Bernard laughed as she walked away. 'What's life all about, if you can't go stark staring bonkers into the grave?'

Troopships came – and went – by the old Empire Dock, but that was a long time ago. Whether the storage sheds by the quay were the ones they had filed through with arms and accoutrements it was impossible to say. Did such buildings last that long in a modern go-ahead world? Bernard wondered.

'I don't remember driving along that motorway to get to town, for a start,' George said.

The revolving tower gave a good view, a silent cargo ship totally unlike the rust-covered tramp steamers plying the Asian trade after the War. The pale blue sky was a shade paler than water, derricks the aerials of triumph over the squalor of human sweat and muscle. A line of forklift trucks parked along the shed testified to the midday heat and the fact that the workers were eating lunch in a bright canteen instead of squatting in their rags over bowls of rice along the warehouse walls. Bernard broke his gaze. 'That was delicious. Let's have another helping.'

The airconditioned greenhouse dome turned almost too slowly to be noticed but suddenly inland an oxblood ziggurat of apartments was framed by the generous greenery of a hill. George speared the spring roll because the bloody thing kept slipping from the sticks. 'It's marvellous to see how far they've pulled themselves up by their own bootstraps.'

Beyond the natural graphline of treetops jutted the vertical success-columns of office blocks, pleasing crenellations against the skyline. 'They're far in advance of Blighty,' Bernard said. 'Not that I begrudge it.'

'They've even got clean water.' George drank some. 'I was talking to a chap who went to India last year. He stayed at first class hotels but daren't clean his teeth at the tap. I'll bet it was drinkable when the British left in forty-nine.'

'Never get anywhere till they've solved the water problem. Still, everything's all right here. If the food's as good as this up country we're in for a right old time.'

'A cushy billet we've fallen into.'

'Good old Jenny. When I think of the way she sprang it on me.'

'We had our work cut out to keep it from you.'

'You pair of rogues. That's what's so good about her. Most people after seven years of marriage stop listening to each other. They have to, I suppose, or go barmy, poor souls. But not me and Jenny. We never stopped listening to each other. Never will, I'm sure. If I stopped listening to her she'd kill me, and if she stopped listening to me I'd kill her. Mind you, it's got to the end between us a few times, when I can't stand any more of the matrimonial roundabout. "I'm leaving," I say. "I've had all I can take." I slam the bedroom door, and fiddle among my shirts so that she'll think I'm packing. But I am. I'm serious. I even drop a tie on my way to the bathroom, in case she doesn't believe me. Not that I could really go, I suppose. But she thinks I might, so she comes in to make sure one way or the other. "One last fuck," I say. "We might as well part amicably." But of course it turns out to be the best fuck for weeks, so how could we part after that? Clears the air at least, but I suspect that one day she'll call my bluff. It'll serve me right if she does – me playing such tricks. But I talk too much. Makes me fancy another beer.'

'That's what we're here for.'

A raised finger, and silently it was brought. 'Even the service is second to none. Smiled at me as well. Did you notice? They don't throw the stuff at you like they do at home. They waste all their energy there on envy and malice. Doesn't make sense.'

'I don't suppose the English ever made good waiters,' George said.

'It's a job like any other.'

'Try telling 'em that.'

'I'd rather not. But I can't think what happened to all the willing and intelligent people there used to be in England. Maybe they were killed in the War. Or they emigrated, and turned into Aussies.' Full circle, and they were back over the Empire Dock. 'I still can't believe it.' Jenny had surprised him for the first time in their married life, and it was not unpleasant, which perhaps was why it was taking so long for the shock to diminish. 'What say we make that trip around the harbour?'

'I'm ready when you are.'

Bumph given out with the twenty-dollar tickets said it was a sailing junk, a few paragraphs of verbal dexterity which nevertheless suggested it might not be. If it had been it would not have got under the Causeway which closed off the inner harbour. The mast had been cut to a stump, an engine installed, and the heat and noise of the city was left behind, a course steered from the mouth of Singapore River and towards a piece of reclaimed land called Peak Island.

George lost count at forty. Or was it fifty? Anyway, rows of yellow plastic chairs were set out on the open deck for the dozen or so people. 'At least we're away from the crowds.' He raked the approaching spit of land with binoculars, while a woman with a man's voice grated on about the ditchwater history of this and that, which comments he could well have done without.

Bernard leaned back in a chair, his mind afloat as the boat would have been had it a sail and the wind dropped. The ambiguous pamphlet galled, though you couldn't take them to court on it, or wouldn't if you had any sense. Making money was part of the sacred instinct, and an Englishman could hardly fault them for plying it. A detachable mast could have been swung up from the horizontal and clamped into position, once they were under the Causeway. But wind power alone would not guarantee a return to the pier in the set time of two hours.

Drifting under sail would have been something to tell Jenny about, cruising silently but for the slide of rope and a squeak of rowlocks (or whatever they were), clean air dusting the body instead of a kerosene reek and the asthmatic gasps of an engine. By sail alone, a gale might have stormed them off course to wrack and ruin on an island of Indonesia – or the Dutch East Indies, as he had known them. Wet sand of the stormlashed beach would have squeezed between his toes. How they had survived he knew not but, wandering from a disconsolate couple who had also swum ashore, he passed palm trees whose heads had been blown inside out like mops, the returning sun warm on his ragged shirt. He came to a paradisal beach, clouds blown clear, the next island a far-off button on the horizon. Palms along the sand were hung with clusters of yellow coconuts, some fallen and ready for eating. The ordeal of shipwreck had tired him, and he fell asleep in the shade knowing he would open his eyes to a sloe-eyed beauty in a sarong, warm breasts pressing close to wake this handsome Englishman stranded on the beach where she took her daily swim.

But she was the emissary of pirates who would hold him for a ransom that never came. Life was cut short. Nightmare revelations spiked the idyll. Their ferocious leader, with cunning brown face, zigzag scar, earring and rotten teeth, jabbed a kris at his ribs with glee, his inhuman roar filling the sky, steely terror shivering up to the universe so that for Bernard there was no escape.

'The hooter's telling us we can go on shore for a twenty-minute shufti,' George said.

'I was having a dream. You look like that bloody old pirate who was about to slit my throat.'

'Sorry I woke you, then.' At the wooden pier an agile old man stood by with a length of rope. Bernard yawned, and slung his camera. 'I thought I'd had my time. A very nasty dream.'

They followed down the gangplank, onto a flattish island of a few acres, a breeze tempering the sour heat. An arched bridge pinched the waist of a pond, never-moving turtles like plates in the small area of murky water. A Chinese temple painted gaudy pinks and yellows looked as if you could break off a piece and eat it. 'A perfect place for beachcombing.'

'I'd go bonkers after a couple of days.' Bernard took a picture of the temple with his almost silent camera. 'Or I'd get toothache.'

'A tent, a few cigars, a couple of dozen books and a radio to get the good old BBC: I'd last out a while, and rest my spirit.'

The passengers seemed to have vanished. A scratch of smoke upped from a caretaker's hut behind the temple. Bernard sat on the parapet. 'Have you ever been on your own for more than forty-eight hours?'

A fair question. 'I'd have to think about it.'

'You wouldn't, if you had.'

'Have you?'

'Only once, when I came home and found my first wife had hopped it. I battened the hatches for three days.'

'Then what did you do?'

'Went and fucked the daylights out of my girlfriend. If I'd gone to her straightaway I'd have been impotent. There was some method in my madness, but that three days lasted forever.'

'Wasn't there anyone else you could have gone to for comfort and consolation?'

He stood, laughing. 'Well, there was my best friend, but he was the one she'd gone off with. Women are like that. Never let your wife meet your best friend.'

A siren signalled from the junk. 'I need to pay a visit before we get back on board,' George said. The toilet cabin was fitted out with sinks and bowls and hand drying machines, and all pipes for the efficient channelling of flush-water, but the floor was gritty with sand. 'In England a place like this wouldn't survive the vandals.'

'He was a wonderful chap, on the face of it, the friend my first wife lit off with. Haven't seen him since. I think he kept out of my way – in fear of his life.' Having finished, he pulled at the urinal division. 'Quite well built.' He was strong from playing squash and doing all manner of exercise twice a week at his club. 'Got to keep up if you want to keep it up. Jenny wouldn't forgive me, and I'd be left without a girlfriend. Must stay faithful now there's Aids around.' Feet against one slab, broad back placed at the next, the veins at his temples took the pressure. A berserker grin crossed his eyes. 'Wonder if I can do it?'

George's old oppo was no novice at vandalism either, having gone his way through public school and been slammed out of university after roistering for eighteen months. When he could get away with it, and a couple of times he had, he had done the same in the army, and now after a lifetime of industrious salesmanship he was about to break up a toilet in a country that, as far as they knew, had harmed no one, having been too busy grinding its way along the sacred motorway of money. 'You've proved your point, merely by wanting to,' George said. 'Now let's be off, or we'll miss the junk.'

But Bernard was too far gone, having recalled a yesteryear injustice to fuel his purpose, flexed his loins, shoes forcefully in front, gathering all his well-fed force as if he had rehearsed for months. He was almost as happy as the mad bastard he had been when on active service, and the NCOs had given up on him as an untouchable who, if they put him on permanent jankers or sent him into the glasshouse, would only emphasize their own failure (as well as lose an excellent soldier) which they wouldn't do because the army looked after its own, at least it did in their regiment. George could do nothing, only watch, in spite of having promised Jenny to keep him in bounds. She knew him better than George, who for years had been out of touch with Bernard's more malign qualities.

Oversanded cement, coated with white enamel, gave with his weight, and cracked the next division also, thumping on to a third and then a fourth, until the whole series of separate pissers turned into a heap of rubble, thus demonstrating, as far as anything could, the domino theory to another north European who came in to empty his bladder, and said with a sour look: 'That should not have been done, England.'

George, about to say: stuff the accusation, switched to temporize. 'It already was. He demolished these unsafe urinals because they constituted a danger to the travelling public. We can't have people cutting their rocks on the jagged bits.'

'Why don't you fuck off and have a gin sling before we sling you into the fucking drink?' Bernard said, quietly.

'We were just having a bit of fun,' George told him. 'High spirits, that's all. Forty years ago we saved these dull industrious buggers from Marxist-Leninist misery.'

Time, he knew, had no meaning to such congenital loonies. Reminiscing about the olden days was a great way to keep the relationship going (for what it was momentarily worth) but to turn thought into action could be positively dangerous in a country where you couldn't argue yourself out of such a situation.

Bernard fastened his zip to a final imperative moan from the boat. 'Don't know what made me do it. Got to keep young, I suppose.'

George couldn't entirely disapprove, when they left the lugubrious man urinating into the wreckage, but they weren't twenty any more, and he was glad when water slopped between the wooden supports of the pier and their departing boat. Unable to doze, he envied Bernard's dreamless features that mirrored a calm soul – until an agitated tremor broke free. George thought of himself as a completed product, shaped and polished by the Master Sculptor called Life, malleable material around a core already hard at birth, certainly by twenty. But Bernard was, as they say, entirely his own man, and quite unshapable, so that there sometimes seemed more periphery than centre, reminding George of a coloured illustration from a children's encyclopaedia of the thirties showing the birth of a heavenly body surrounded by molten rock and fire.

George, as he knew only too well, had all his life retreated further and further into the refuge of himself, as protection against the ever assiduous shaper of his soul, till there seemed no periphery left. But at least his soul was his own. Or was it? Was anybody's? And if not, in whose possession was it? Coming on such a jaunt he hardly knew who he was. Well, maybe he never had known, except in those far-off days when to wonder who he was hadn't occurred to him. From the eternal defender of himself against the tribulations of being alive, when he wondered who he was, he became lost in an inhospitable continent of speculation, where the only question rotting him from the middle was why he should ask any questions at all.

One island turned up after another, but the passengers

had lost interest. A free fruit drink was given out. The distant skyscrapers of Singapore, a clump to the north, a gaggle to the south, sometimes as if at all points of the compass, were an achievement for a small country with no resources except the sea, tourism, and a genius for banking. It helped, and maybe it was everything, that the people were orderly, industrious and intelligent. They did not have to wonder who they were, and as such could only inherit the earth.

four

The airbus struck out over the mangroves of Johore, up through seven miles of sky, nothing visible but pearls of moisture at the windows. Power provides the speed that keeps the weight afloat through empty air: Bernard loved the lift it gave his spirit, but found it hard to guess what Jenny was doing at home – sleeping, most likely – or to fix his imagination on the geography of the office.

Nothing existed beyond such an aeroplane, neither past nor future, which he supposed was the same for the other passengers looking at the back of the seat in front. He remembered the same trip in a clapped-out Dakota, twenty-odd swaddies instead of three hundred on board, flying time three hours instead of one, a mile up rather than six.

Booze could not be served while overflying a Moslem country – it seemed – but George drew a flask from his travelling bag, and passed it over, so that Bernard's cake-walking throat caused a look of disgust and hatred from a man across the gangway wearing a white pillbox hat, stubble greying his chin, leanness incarnate. He gave a long stare back, then turned to George. 'They must think they own the goddamned world.'

'They soon will, if we aren't careful.' He took a gannet-like swig. 'The bloody sky, as well.'

'Liberty or death!' Bernard cried. 'Send a gunboat.'

'Make it two,' George said. 'Cheers!'

'Cheers! We'll have to, sooner or later. Here's to the Brylcreem Boys!'

'Roll out the Gatling guns!' Well, why not? Who could be serious at a time like this?

Over Malacca the mist cleared, dark green against a sea of whitish blue. These days there were no ships, Bernard uneasy at emptiness beginning where the land stopped. A plane moved and the earth rolled slowly under in spite of your apparent speed. Planes had travelled at not much more than a hundred, but soon you would go from London to Sydney in a couple of hours. Poor old George looked a bit pale, from too much guzzling at Woolsthorpe Circle. Didn't feel too good himself. The food was so wonderful you couldn't stop eating. And why not? At the point of death he would shed tears for the food he hadn't been able to eat, wine not drunk, women not loved, scenery not witnessed. Being sixty, he might not live to be eighty. Or he would die in the next five minutes. From being too old to die young, he was suddenly too old to die at all.

'I'm the only one allowed to be lugubrious,' George responded. The cellophane covering his cake wouldn't come apart where it was supposed to. Impossible to get an incision with finger nails. Nor did his teeth make any impression. In fact he nearly lost his dental plate. Look fine, scrabbling for that up the gangway soaked in whisky. His army jackknife was deep in the bag under his feet.

Bernard had similar trouble, extracted his cake in four pieces. 'They gave us paper napkins, at least.'

A hostess helped George, the paper separating as if on oiled zips. 'It must be paradise to marry one of 'em.'

Bernard thought the matter through. 'She'd be a dab hand at opening a packet of cake, but in ten years she'd be just like the wife you'd ditched to marry her.'

'I'd be dead by then, so it wouldn't matter.'

'You might not be so lucky. Going native's not for us.' The coffee was mouthwash, but it swilled the cake from his fillings. 'Twenty-year-old backpackers do it in Bali, till mummy and daddy cut them off without a penny. Or the locals get fed up with them. The only place where we could hang out for a high time would be Bangkok. A friend who stayed a week on his way to Oz got a couple of Thai girls to move in with him. Nothing they wouldn't do, he said. Never-never land, really. Maybe we'll go next time.'

The stewardess who collected their cups no doubt reflected what a happy pair they were. Neither looked their age – Bernard assumed – except George maybe, nose at the window and waiting for the island to drift onto the radar screen.

A man and woman could be married thirty years, George mused – scanning the endless blue plate of water – and become like icebergs in order to stay together, one-tenth of each in communication while the other nine-tenths seethed in opposition underneath, though what was wrong with that if the species were to continue? 'Why,' Gladys had said, 'you're having a mid-life crisis. A bit late, of course, but then, you always were a bit late in everything, as well I know.' And he had said nothing, grey eyes shining, not giving in to the sweet retaliation of telling her about his casual affairs with her friends, for fear of hearing her say she had always known about them (and in any case hadn't been behindhand with his friends) and then he would have the satisfaction of keeping back the secrets of those she had not known about, fully realizing that she was doing the same. Such pressure no longer existed, though it was peculiar that he felt more stress at the heart now than during years of agonizing quarrels.

You only knew what someone was thinking if you could guess what they were refusing to say, so it was impossible to know whether or not you were right. You had to be satisfied with that, because life was a galley, and you kept on keeping on, happiness when wind filled the sails and sun lent a momentary warmth to the slog. And in those moments of happiness, with donkey shades over the eyes, you forgot the anguish, and continued to hope because there was no choice, since if you attempted in a moment of anguish to banish the anguish forever you would realize your fatal mistake when anguish rushed back in spite of everything. Still, if men and women weren't made for living together, who was?

'They're the animated version of the five-fingered widow.' Bernard had words for everything, not much he hadn't experienced. 'But what's worse than the five-fingered widow is when those same hot little fingers belong to a hand that goes off with your money.'

George identified Muong by the smaller island to the southeast, where the old leper colony used to be. He saw the bridge which now ran across to the mainland, and wondered if there were any lepers left in this modern supercharged version of Malaysia, apart from the moral pair who were about to land.

Gravel along the underbelly of the plane, and a couple of barely credible bumps, signified that they had come to earth. Coconut palms and banana trees, with native huts between, bordered the single runway.

The usual steam heat met them on the steps. 'No red carpet for the great liberators,' Bernard chaffed. 'A band and a few dancing girls wouldn't be out of place. They've forgotten our valiant fight for their welfare.'

Queues at police and immigration soon dissolved, a smart young woman in khaki to stamp their passports. They stood by the conveyor waiting for luggage. 'Better scratch that white powder from your finger nails. I don't want to take you home in a plastic bag,' George said. 'The perfect smugglers would look like us. Now we know how to do it.'

'We would be caught first time,' Bernard said. 'On holiday in Italy last year they had a half-ton sniffer dog at Pisa airport watching the bags come on the conveyor, all set to salivate at pot, hash, coke, speed, crack or mary-jane. Didn't find a thing, but near the end of its search the incontinent hound lumbered up onto the roundabout, lifted a by-no-means inconsiderable limb of a fifth leg, and performed a prolonged act of micturition against a rather posh piece of luggage. Not mine, I might say. But it made the handler's day.'

George picked his case off the moving platform.

'Can't think why yours always arrives before mine. You must know somebody,' Bernard said.

'Didn't you see her wink when we booked in at Singapore?'

'You made a date for Bangkok, I suppose.' He gazed into the distance as pieces of luggage were taken away. 'Looks like I'm going to be last, as usual.'

A single brown suitcase came around the bend. 'Is that yours?'

'It had better be.' He lifted it half way, and let it fall.

'Maybe there's more to come,' George said.

'There's no one else waiting.' He was bereft, as the same brown suitcase elbowed on its solitary round once more. 'I think the unmentionable's happened, and some bastard's walked off with my kit.'

'Are you certain this one isn't yours?'

He stopped it with his foot. 'Mine has two wheels at the back. How anybody could make such a mistake I'll never know.' When the bag came round again he picked it up. 'At least we've got something to bargain with.'

'I'd drop it, if I were you,' George said quietly. 'It's the oldest trick in the world. If someone wants to get a load of drugs through the customs all he does is pick up a case similar to his and let somebody else carry the hot stuff through. Not knowing what they've got, they look all innocent and have no trouble. Afterwards, the smuggler stops him outside and says: "You've got my case, old chap. So sorry I made a mistake. Let's swop 'em back. Hope I didn't inconvenience you. Come and have a drink with me sometime." Nearly got yourself hanged, you crazy old fool!'

Bernard, losing nine-tenths of his tan, leaned against a pillar to recover from the close call. 'What a perfectly villainous notion.'

'We'd better tell the baggage clerk you've lost your tackle.' A uniformed airline woman led them towards the main doors, and the chatting customs men let George and his luggage through without a gesture. They descended via a flight of steps to her office, and sat down. Would they like a drink? No, they'd just had coffee on the aeroplane. 'We were cared for superbly,' Bernard said. 'It was the most wonderful service, second to none. So hard to imagine my luggage being lost.'

'You must give me five minutes.'

George was always amazed at how well Bernard's neanderthal charm took effect, expecting him to be frostily told that women weren't to be treated like that in the modern world. No doubt if he got such a retort he would handle it in such a debonair fashion that he would not be the discomfited party.

She smiled. 'I'll go and see what I can do. In the meantime, gentlemen' (she really did say gentlemen) 'please make yourselves comfortable. And don't worry, Mr Missenden.'

'Looks like your troubles will soon be over.'

'I have high hopes. Strange how the more beautiful a person is the nicer they are.'

'She's gone,' George said. 'And the room's not wired.'

'As far as we know. But I'm serious. When I'm loony I'm loony, but when I'm serious I'm really serious. You should know that by now.'

'I do.' True enough. But Bernard was fundamentally loony enough to think he was being serious when in fact he was at his most loony, and though when he was loony there might be an element of seriousness in it, the looniness undoubtedly lurked and he expected you to appreciate it.

Perhaps most people were serious all their lives, and only rarely let out a flash of looniness, but Bernard had an aspect of total looniness that revealed a gleam of seriousness now and again, as if to let you see how genuine his looniness was, but also to hint at the profundity of his serious side. And if by and large Bernard had got on in the world, which his income certainly indicated, it was because his looniness was not only in tune with much of the world's, and of the sort that people appreciated on certain occasions, and remembered him favourably by, but because he knew how to control it. He ought by these uncertainties to have been a person few people would trust, but in fact he was held to be more solid and reliable than many who were far less loony and who merely tried to deceive by their seriousness. He was recognized as a stalwart for the firm he worked for, being not only assiduous in business, but entertaining in leisure, at a time when few could, with apparent sincerity, be both.

'From now on, I'll carry a clean shirt in my hold-all. It's a matter of live and learn, I suppose.' He had been in a similar situation before, but couldn't remember where or when. You can't even learn by experience if your memory goes on the blink, and in any case so many things can go wrong that if you rely on experience to teach you you never stop learning, so that you wouldn't have time to do anything else, and what kind of a life would that be? You often have to have an experience two or three times before it sticks. 'I remember Jenny telling me to keep a shirt and socks with me at all times, but I simply couldn't imagine my case going astray.' He stretched his legs, well at ease. 'I'll buy some togs in the morning if the case isn't back by then.'

She walked smiling to her desk. 'Your luggage is at the Golden Pagoda Hotel, on the other side of the island. We phoned the careless gentleman, and it will be back with you as soon as possible.'

'Tomorrow?'

'Oh no, this evening.'

Bernard was ready to go. 'Sounds a first-rate bit of detective work.'

'Like Sherlock Holmes?' she suggested.

He went back from the door to shake her hand. 'I'm extremely grateful, and so sorry that you've been put to so much trouble.'

'It's all part of our service.'

'We're staying at the Home and Colonial Hotel, so I wonder if you would care to have dinner with me tonight?'

'That's very kind,' she said, 'but I must go back to Singapore.'

George led the way to the taxi line, sweat breaking out of the skin like ants getting up and on the move. 'You had a bloody cheek.'

'I had to show my appreciation,' he laughed. 'Anyway, she might have said yes. You know the hoary one about the man who stands on a street corner and asks any goodlooking woman if she'll go to bed with him? He gets quite a lot of snubs, not to say slaps, but he also gets a satisfactory number of acceptances.'

George, luggage weightier the more you handled it, slowed down. 'I don't think that kind of behaviour would pass muster here. After all, it's Kung-Fu Land we've dropped into out of the skies.'

'It was Fuck-You Land last time we were here,' Bernard smiled, turning to wait. 'Couldn't care less Land. Fuck you Jack I'm all right Land. Except for your mates, of course. Covering fire was everything.'

The same thatched huts between the palms, food stalls in the kampongs, and open garages to take care of the motor-bikes that hadn't been on the roads before. Everything was more squalid and go-ahead, hotter than they remembered. Whereas the air had been previously tempered by the reek of mangroves from the mainland, now through the open window came odours of dust and petrol, the taxi warping and wefting in a gangland of traffic, avoiding lorries and buses and trishaws, and pedestrians crossing the white line of the road. The taxi was also overtaken by the dodgery of countless small powered motorbikes, some perilously laden, and how a few didn't go slithering to disaster Bernard never knew. He laughed at the near misses, the apparent chaos of the two-way river mixing at the middle of the road, but never faltering in its purpose of getting people from A to B and – with luck he supposed – back again. 'There used to be nothing in this area but banana groves.'

'I know,' George said. 'We walked here once.'

'Did we?'

'Wandered off the road, went half a mile through the elephant grass, and when we got to a hut we asked a Malay to sell us some bananas. They were on trees all around, and we could have reached up and taken a few, but in those days we were honest as well as loony – a funny combination. He was delighted to let us have a whole branch of little pink ones for a few cents, and we ate 'em on the way back to the ferry.' Most of the others had been camp hounds or beaten trackers: over on the ferry for steak and egg at the Boston Café and a few dances at the City Lights – but he and Bernard often wandered along the beach sign-talking to Tamil fishermen, or they would trek into the forest in the hope of finding what they didn't know they were looking for.

'And now look at it. Villas, apartment houses, even highrise blocks. We must be getting into town. Changed a bit less than Singapore, though.'

Traffic coagulated at the lights, and turnings led among two-storeyed buildings and the same homely shabby streets and shop fronts opening onto the pavements, most of them unaltered and seemingly unlicked by paint, though several generations of it had presumably licked and gone since then. Dust and noise, and smells from exhaust pipes overrode the homelier odours of dung fires and rotting fruit.

The Home and Colonial Hotel was a hundred years old,

ancient for such a town. Bernard showed his passport at the desk. 'Clever Jenny, for getting us into a place like this.'

A girl in a smart costume found the reservation form and handed George the key. 'Time for a shower,' he said. 'Then down to dinner.' From the room behind, the intermittent clack of a manual typewriter sounded like waterdrops from an overful gutter in a rainstorm.

'Everything would be perfect,' Bernard said to the girl, 'if I hadn't lost my luggage.'

'It often happens,' she said. 'If it arrives during dinner, sir, I'll let you know.'

They were not allowed to carry a suitcase, or work the lift to the second floor, where their large wood-panelled room overlooked the terrace and the Straits. The façade of the hotel along the waterfront was painted yellow, with terracotta eaves, balconies on the central part of the first floor, otherwise plain windows for all three storeys. Wooden slatted chairs and tables were set to one side of the green-surfaced swimming pool.

There were two large beds, a desk, and clothes cupboards running the length of one end. Airconditioning sounded like an idling Spitfire engine, but you soon got used to it. In the sitting area a low glasstopped table and a couple of armchairs faced the television and an (empty, Bernard said, closing it) refrigerator. The large bathroom had a high window opening onto the noise of traffic and crows, such an unadorned room you would think it had been wheeled up and tacked on from another kind of establishment. 'I need a slug of whisky to steady my nerves,' he said.

'Me too, if you don't mind.'

He got glasses from the bathroom. 'Water?'

'Neat.'

'Might as well get ready for my soak.' In his pants Bernard was straight and solid fleshed, not lean exactly, but with little to spare. 'Cheers, then.'

'Let's live forever.'

'Longer, I hope. Where would we be without the odd shot of firewater, do you suppose?'

George relished the hot flood into his stomach, smacked his slight overhang of a belly. 'Reading our Bible in Misery Lane. God bless the stuff!' But God would not bless it, if God there was, though God there had to be if you had such a thought.

Off the large reception court, where circling fans at the ceiling gave a touch of olden times, was a dining room, a bar, breakfast room, and a ballroom. Outside, an esplanade fronted the water, a view to the straight coast of the mainland. A dozen huge black eighteenth-century cannon were deployed between palm trees along the walk, muzzles pointing as if for a last-ditch defence of the rich against the poor. A squat evil-looking bombard had somehow found its way among them, wide maw tilted to the sky as if the first shot that went up would come straight down and blow the hotel to bits.

Several brown-skinned young women played in the pool, while a party of tanned European men sat at a slatted table, two with the insignia of air force officers on the shoulders of their khaki shirts, silent with their beer, as if they had already said everything of importance either to the world or themselves.

The opposite shore was darkening, sea grey under mellowing yellow light. George trawled up and down with binoculars, trying to make out where the old camp had been.

'If you spot it, let me know.'

'I've fixed it pretty well, I think. The huts aren't there any more. Some apartments have been built.'

Bernard relished a pre-dinner beer. 'Can you see *me*? I mean, as I was then.'

'Of course I can.'

'What am I doing?'

'The usual. Sitting on the basha steps with a bottle of

Van der Hum plonk. Blotted out of your mind, by the look of it. Now you're waving the empty bottle. Oh my God!'

'What did I do?'

'The sergeant came to say we're moving out on patrol, to chase the bandits, and . . .'

'I don't believe it.'

'You hit him with the bottle. Now you're for it. Blood's running down his astonished face.'

'Well, it would be, wouldn't it?' Bernard put both hands to his head. 'Don't tell me any more. I can't take it. I've become more civilized since those days.'

'He's marching back from the guardroom with a couple of six-foot redcaps. You're fighting drunk. You're killing 'em. No, they're killing you. They're putting all four boots in. Now you've gone stiff. You're on their shoulders like a log of wood. The colonel's arrived. He's shouting at them though, not you. You seem sober now, almost contrite, if that's possible. The colonel's asking you to get back in the jungle to have another crack at the bandits. You're the best tracker he's got, he says. He's patting you on the shoulder, offering you a smoke from his cigarette case. He wants you for the sports competition next week as well. What a charmed life you lead.'

'I'm ashamed of myself.' Bernard leaned his forehead against a clenched fist and began to sob. 'I promise to reform because, well, things just can't go on like this. Life is too short to sin forever, and to have the DTs at twenty is nothing short of tragic.' Then he straightened, and slugged off the rest of his beer. 'But what are *you* doing?'

The men at the next table were puzzled at such chaps carrying on like a pair of sprightly actors. The young can act the fool and be amusing, George thought, but grown men only embarrass any unlucky spectators. But he said: 'Sitting on my charpoy reading a library book. No, I've put it away, because Tom Parsons, my best pal – after your good self, of course – has brought his board over for a game of chess. Oh how nice a lad I was!'

Bernard simulated bitterness. 'Butter wouldn't melt up your arse.'

Continuing his scrutiny of the opposite shore George saw palm trees packed behind a paler string of beach, a barrier broken by apartment blocks painted the colour of dried blood. The deca-magnification brought the coast close yet never sharp enough in detail. Nothing moved, no signs given, the area remote and dead, though it was undoubtedly where they had put up their tents forty years ago. But the 'undoubtedly' was doubtful in its sincerity, too pat to mean much. He didn't know, couldn't tell. Never would know, most likely, so he wondered why he was here, or at least why, being here, he could not simply feel enjoyment and drop this bogus search for some connection to the past. The warm breeze lifted cooler air from pockets over the water. His appetite at least was real.

Happiness was the ability to overprint the past with the present, merge them into harmony so as to give meaning to life, but his attempt brought an unpleasant feeling that he was too old, the gap too wide, that he knew too much. The blokes of all those years ago, himself among them, would say: 'Look at him now! The miserable old sinner is too mean even to smile at himself in the mirror. He never learned how to stop life knocking him around.'

'Wonderful,' Bernard said, 'just to sit here. I don't think I've felt such peace for ages.'

George went for the Colonial type menu at fifty-five dollars: Dutch pea soup; followed by a steak, gammon, chicken and sausage grill; then trifle. 'Many things alter, but the grub seems to stay the same.'

'The old *nasi-goreng*'s still got an egg on top,' Bernard said, after his soup and spring rolls. 'Not too hot for a first class hotel, so maybe we'll eat from the street tomorrow.

Bound to be good in a town like this. That Colonial-style crap you're eating's too heavy for me.'

'It's delicious. How's your greasy sludge?'

'Hardly what one might call fuckers grub, though I expect it's nourishing enough to yank down the odd palm tree or two.' A three-piece combo gave out 'The Eton Boating Song' mildly jazzed up, which would certainly have been played forty years ago. 'I expect the place was full of planters and travellers then, military and local highlife. Lots of hobnobbing and fornicating. Shame it's so dead at the moment.'

George signalled for more beer. 'It's not the season yet. In a couple of months the Aussies will be up by the thousand. Lovely big-bosomed Aussie women padding around in bare feet.'

'And big beer-bellied Aussie men who would get very pissed off if you so much as looked at them. Anyway, they go up the coast, to the new hotels with their own beaches.' He plied chopsticks as if born to them. 'In the old days I kept a notebook to scribble in, and I brought it back out with me.'

'I often wished I'd kept one. Never occurred to me. Too busy lying on the beach.'

'I even found a poem in it.'

'Another joke?' George said.

'Well, I was made to write them at my posh school.'

'So was I, at my grammar school, but I didn't make a habit of it.'

'It could be,' Bernard said, looking back on their early friendship as a miracle, 'that we were just that bit more civilized than we remember.'

George mopped up the last outposts of his grill. Landing in Malaya from the unhappy state of austerity Britain had no doubt inspired many to poetic ruminations, though few as far as putting them into script. The waiter apologized at the lack of trifle for dessert, so he settled for a dish of iced lychees, hoping it might make up for the dearth of vegetables.

'I'll read it to you.' Bernard brought up a worn buff notebook from his bag, the cover decorated with overinked but fading shields and serpents, headstones and naked women. 'I'm glad I drew them like this, instead of having them tattooed on my chest and arms like a cave dweller. My outside outside and my inside inside is what I've always believed in. But I came across the book in an old trunk the other day with my uniform, kukri, and a few other odds and ends.'

He would never have resurrected the matter if he had thought it had any connection with him now. But there were many mansions in the house of youth, life chopping them off one by one till you were left with the bleak cell of your one-roomed mind in post middle age, an electric cell nonetheless, with more bursts of energy and troubling intuitions than in those thousand rooms of youth put together.

His smile implied it was only a joke that he had scribbled the lines at all, something you could therefore share with your lifelong friend, who seemed too much of an introvert to let go of his thoughts this evening. 'God knows why I wrote it, but listen:

Everything in the jungle is more timid than you except
  the tiger;
Everything in the jungle retreats at your advance except
  the vegetation;
Everything in the jungle swallows its silence except the
  river:
Everything that happens says the jungle never changes.'

George tapped the table, shook the phlegm around in his throat while waiting for coffee. 'Very profound. You've got the feeling exactly. I can smell the place, though I never forgot that, anyway. But your lines bring back the soul of it. Little did I suspect what you were up to when you stood on guard by the camp gate. Did you do any more?'

He looked down, a peculiar smile. 'The odd ditty. I

suppose it made a change from harrying bandits.' He read the poem to himself with half ashamed fascination, slowly as if each word was a brick smashing windows to get at the dimly displayed goods of his past, as if he couldn't believe he had written the poem either, but was unable to stop something more powerful than himself from informing whatever was left of his unspoilt soul that he must have, and it gave him an expression of fragile belief, close to pleasure, that George had never before seen on his well contained features. The credence of his having been utterly different, even to the person he thought he remembered, was cleaned away by a sudden smile. 'I must have copied it from a travel book of the time, to send to one of my girlfriends. What a crafty young devil I must have been. Funny how one never changes.'

Too hot to stroll, they hired a pedicab at ten dollars for an hour. 'Three times more than he should get,' Bernard said, 'but what the hell? Let's make his day.'

'Oh no, sir,' said the man, very friendly, 'it's a good price, special for you.'

He laughed. 'Let's go then, you old rogue.'

The fragile contraption sagged under them. With everything so cheap George thought it their duty to circulate the cash, for in spite of highrise flats and proliferating traffic they were still in a Third World country. The man stood on a pedal, total weight to get his machine from the kerb. Shop fronts were down, only restaurants still lit at their late evening business. The meat of memory had no taste, he wasn't here, couldn't say he was even part of himself. 'Recognize anything?'

Bernard peered. 'Same shabby place under all the glitter. More motorbikes, of course.'

And no sign of malnutrition, a group of the poorest sort scoffing themselves silly at a cookstall. Still, George felt pity for the huff-puffing pedicab-wallah – he almost said 'coolie' – transporting a pair of well-fed Europeans on a sightseeing tour around a place they had known like the back of their hands. The man might be happy to earn more than he had made all day, but George had to resist looking at his watch in the hope that more of the hour had gone by. The poor chap was about forty, hard to imagine he would get to forty-five, his heart would burst or his lungs go bang, but maybe he was saving to get the downpayment on a taxi so that he could join the queue of those already waiting all hours by the hotel for a single fare that would also make their day, though for some it might never come because too many were competing, like the pedal pushers squatting on the pavement, envious at his fare of two foreigners who would pay six times what he got from the local matron he ferried to the market every morning. George poked him in the back. 'Get down for a while.'

The street light seemed unwilling to overshine, the man's face wary of giving much expression. George forced himself to look at his short black hair swept back, forehead globuled with sweat, mouth open in heavy breathing to show discoloured teeth, an almost-pauper dressed in the rag of a soaked vest.

'What's going on?' Bernard stayed in his seat, but gave a jerk of the head, as if they had somewhere to go and would be late.

'I'm taking over.' They turned into a less interesting street, potholes lurching them sideways, dodging some maniac driver hopped up on rice wine or pot.

The man grinned. 'What you say, sir?'

'I'm going to drive this boneshaker for a bit.'

Darkness, the smell of dying fires and food gone slightly rotten drifted across his nostrils. George smiled as if it might make his decision more acceptable. They threaded a confluence of brighter lights, a posse of motorcyclists cutting their track. Ever willing to please, perhaps get a bigger tip, the man steered to the pavement. 'You want to look on buildings, sir? Shops not open till morning, but the buildings are very interesting.'

'I'm going to ride the bloody thing.'

Bernard's shouts stopped an old man shuffling up the street, wispy beard twirling like a water diviner. 'Now I know why we called you Raving Rhoads. Stark staring bonkers!' He stood up to wave. 'Drive on, Mactosh, off to the City Lights, brothel of brothels and Babylon United. Let's get as stuck in as we've never been stuck in before!'

Drunk as he was, the ultimate lark, round the bend and halfway up the zigzags, and even if there was no excuse, he would do what he had to do because he wasn't drunk enough not to do it, looking on at himself, separated from the scene by sufficient booze to see the beaten down foot pumping pedicab driver, clapped out and breathless, him seeing George as such a fool that George had no option but to mount the saddle for a jaunt through the town.

'Sir, please, sir!' the driver cried.

'Get out of the way, you pimp. Tried to sell your sister, eh?' Such words and others burst like the foulest of blisters, shouted in fun as if they had been picked up from the mother's milk of the earth they had lived in. He heard himself and loathed himself, when all he wanted was to feel the effort, rob the man even of what he suffered to prove that he could endure it as well, and afterwards to say how easy it had been, so that he would not feel ashamed at having been pedalled around the streets. Oh George, you silly old fool, I've got your number right enough, George said.

His whole weight on a single pedal wouldn't move it from midday to the bottom of the clock, though he stood hard on one foot, wriggling the other leg at all angles to show what a joke it was. From feeling ludicrous he faced humiliation. Half a dozen people watched the show, but he urged himself on, a twenty-year-old from the camp across the water gone completely off his trolley, blind drunk and out to break any limb that got in his way.

'Take brake off, sir,' the driver said.

His shirt had been dropped in water and flopped back to find the folds of his body. Tubal Cain in the foundry was using his heart as an anvil. He gripped the sticky handlebars. The poor bastard's life was a machine to beat the blood out of his heart when chance gave him the privilege of a fare, living on a handful of rice and shrimps, and kipping in the corner of a shed somewhere. Muscles in gear, he would know what it was like, his head a lantern immersed in sweat as the pedal descended, and the flimsy vehicle moved to an embarrassing cheer from bystanders.

'For God's sake, I'll be seasick.' Bernard laughed at the man trotting along. 'Sir, sir!' – fearful to lose his awful bloody – George recalled his father's dread word for it – 'livelihood', a man's livelihood, without which it was surely a plunge into destitution, all self-respect gone, nothing remaining but death and putrition.

He struggled to avoid the peril of traffic which, noting the spectacle, sounded their gloating horns as the pedicab swayed wide to take a corner, a vision of its arse turned to the sky from a monsoon ditch, and him – not to say Bernard – with arms and legs manglespread on the pavement. He smiled, because insurance taken out at the airport could only land them in the best clinic. Juddering wheels missed the six-foot-deep mini-moat, and he tacked a course in the middle of the street, victory powering his soles, except that after a hundred more yards such victory seemed irrelevant due to the gate of his heart shutting over and over to block off his view of the dingy buildings.

A sickness at the stomach linings forced him upright, afraid to move an eyelid, the vehicle freewheeling towards the kerb till it came to a stop. A cooling rain pressed a dishcloth to his forehead, another on the flesh of his skull. Sandals flapped close, and he wanted to feel asphalt under him, but daren't try because his arms were snakes wriggling from his body, legs likewise tapping the pedals, telling himself to hold still, hold still, trying to make every limb obey his brain and come slowly back into his sphere of control.

Bernard gripped his arm. 'Let's have you down.' The owner stood, passive but with eyes fierce, unable to help or complain. He knelt to look at the wheels.

'It's my lungs,' George said. 'Stitch, I think.'

'You're crazier than me. I'd never have thought it.'

Legs became solid, and he could see more clearly, no longer that faint sick feeling at the guts. The green park at the end of the street was a desirable place to be, to lie on the grass when he got there and never move again. 'I'll sleep under the trees.'

'It's back to the hotel for you.' Bernard turned to the driver. 'Come on, Johnny, fun's over. Get into harness, and no pratting about. The hour's nowhere up yet.' He levered George into his seat, and cracked a whip as if along a line of huskies. 'You're too old, always were, except for that little bit of jungle-bashing when you were twenty. Lifting and humping's for the others, not us. We weren't made for it, never were.'

Lights like needles pushing his eyes shut, stomach without a base, brain gone to the Sago Sea. He pulled the flesh at his cheek, felt a tear under his eye at the pain. But it eased the ache in his left arm. 'That showed him, though,' he turned to Bernard. 'I can carry the burden as well as anybody.'

'He's thirty years younger. But what a sight! I'll never forget. It's something to write to Jenny about. She'd call us a pair of liars if we had no adventures to relate.'

George's heartbeats settled into their normal rate. 'As for you wrecking that bog in Singapore, I never saw such blatant vandalism.'

'And you nearly smashed this Heath Robinson contraption to bits, you mad bastard.'

The driver turned at George's hyena laugh, dreading more mischief from these pink-skinned unpredictable barbarians who had more money to spend in a week than he came by in a year. What he had done was not quite done, George knew, feeling daft at having failed to prove himself a good hauler of human merchandise. Yet he had broken the rules by playing the grand nabob in doing as he bloody well liked, then acted the penitent by assuming the burden of the poor and dispossessed, like some researcher on what hard labour was all about – only to discover that it fuddled his brain and made his body helpless with fatigue.

'Nearly killed yourself.' Bernard sounded envious at such an outlandish exploit. 'What next, I wonder?'

'A shower,' George said, as they drew up at the hotel. 'And a chota peg for a nightcap.' He took out his wallet. 'I'll give him one extra. He's been a good sport.'

'We've only had fifty minutes, and you did half of the work!'

The man stared at his eleven dollars, more than he had been promised, but not enough; even more than he had expected, but it ought to be more. 'You pay for the damage, sir?'

'Can't see a scratch.' George looked to make sure. 'Perfect condition, Johnny.'

He stroked a mudguard, hoping to find something, even an old dent.

'You can't blame him for trying it on.' Bernard took George's arm, seeing him hesitate. 'But he's been well paid.'

The man protested further, and Bernard walked back. 'Enough! Piss off!' Wind shifted the palm branches around like paper. 'You have to be firm.' He walked towards the desk. 'Otherwise they'll never give us a fair ride again. I don't mind paying double, or even treble, but we don't have to throw it away.'

George's aches were either diminishing, or he was getting used to them. A youngster could prank without being a fool, but not a man of sixty. 'In the old days we only walked when we had to. We swam, or we rowed on the water where it was cool. Otherwise we were far too sensible to exert ourselves.'

'We're loonier now than we were then,' Bernard said. 'Or maybe in those days we weren't loony at all. We were young, so we had too much to lose.' He took the key from the immaculately dressed young woman. 'Could be that young people are never really foolish, anyway. They just lark around to learn and get experience. That's why the old let them get away with it. I've always had a soft spot for the young, even when I was young myself.'

'Excuse me, sir,' the receptionist said, 'but your case has been taken to your room.'

'What efficiency! Now I can change my shirt. Has the other chap got his yet?'

'It is still at the airport. He'll have to fetch it himself in the morning.'

'Good! Serve him right,' he said, turning her smile into a laugh. 'What delightful people you all are!' He was happy that the misplacement of his luggage had given him the chance to fraternize with this lovely Asian woman. 'All's well that ends well. That's Shakespeare, by the way.'

'I know, sir. I've read some of his beautiful works.'

'Bless you,' he said. 'Goodnight to all you fair ladies.'

'Goodnight, sir.'

'Flights of angels guard you to your rest.'

'Hamlet, sir?'

'Certainly, my dear.'

'Oh, for God's sake,' George said.

Bernard took his arm and led him towards the lift. 'No, old boy, for mine. I hope to get there yet. Say no more. As for the suitcase, you have to be right about that sleight of hand. I expect the hotel denizens of the northern coast will be stoned out of their minds for the next fortnight. Our cases weren't so similar for such a mix-up.'

George stayed in the lobby, intending to observe people going back and forth, but he was soon copiously sweating, the night heat as steamy as the day's. No one was about, in any case, for some adventure of body and soul which would see him into heaven or the other place. Either would have been welcome, the way he felt.

So he went upstairs back to the airconditioned room, to clink a last glass with Bernard before bedtime, the one godlike sound, they both agreed, that helped you to sleep, and milled out the best of dreams. It was certainly true that when George lay down his heart no longer ached.

five

His chair was facing the window. 'The sky's covered with alto-cumulus.'

Bernard chopped into his bacon and eggs. Only in places like this, and in the north of England, he supposed, did you get fried bread. 'How come you know the names of all the clouds?'

'When I took a class on a field trip and one of the kids asked: "What are those funny shaped things in the sky called, sir?" I had to be able to give an answer.' Clusters of fat coconuts hung under the canopies of palms along the promenade. The opposite shore was visible across a sea of inky grey. 'I still can't make out where the old camp was.'

'Hidden by the trees, I expect. One day soon we'll go over and do a recce.' Bernard hardly wanted to. What was the hurry? He had heard it said that you can't go home again, or back again, and for decades had thought it wasn't so, that you could in fact do what the hell you liked. But he was beginning to see that that applied only insofar as you were young, in which case it made little difference whether you went back or not because you were then, after all, not very far from the point to which you might care to go back, so that it didn't feel necessary to go back. But at sixty, wanting to go back signified that you were getting old, and he should have known better than to betray himself by coming here, except that it had been Jenny's idea. Still, here he was, the sojourn a godsent opportunity to take it easy, of which he felt in more need the longer the holiday went on. 'Just going up to use the bathroom.'

George stayed to finish his tea, and to smoke. The woman at the next table wore a white high-collared blouse, an ecclesiastical type cravat over her bosom, a greying pink-skinned woman somewhere in her thirties. He looked, while not appearing to, at her turning the menu around and wondering whether to go continental or have an English fry-up, and decided she was very personable, as English a beauty as you could get, the high forehead and florid cheeks redeemed by lips as exquisitely shaped as on any painting, an ultra-civilized bow suggesting both the sensible and the vulnerable, an aspect not quite matching the rest of her Home Counties features. He had seen it in other women, but didn't care to recall their names because she was enough to fill any man with satisfying speculation.

A black and orange moggie, thin as a rake, a truncated tail as if a crow had swept off with the bigger part of it, went warily by the open door, the arteries of its arse outlined like a Chinese lantern in the dark. With an inward sigh, and a surreptitious fart, he got up from the breakfast table, a curt good morning nod as he passed her by, beyond the door before knowing whether or not she responded, but carrying with him the picture of a friendly smile, and the fact that he could fall in love with those lips alone – wondering why he hadn't noticed any of this in the glimpse of her at Heathrow.

Strange that in such heat – condensation without the air being wet – they should have the energy to walk. The middle of town hadn't altered, though they recalled nothing specific. 'If it had,' George said, 'we might have remembered more.'

Forty years ago there were less than half as many people on the island, and you could see how calm and empty the streets had been from old photographs. Nowadays the air was fouled by cars and motorbikes. Crows, barely noticed then, had multiplied. Openfronted shops displayed spectacles, cameras, socks, hats, luggage, watches. 'All the machine-made necessities of the modern world,' Bernard said. 'Junk for the hoi polloi.' He bought a canvas haversack at four dollars to keep his cash and camera in.

'I expect those very meaty Chinese stoogies I used to smoke in the old days went out with the Flood,' George said.

'Like the lovely taxi-dancers from the City Lights. We'd buy a strip of fifty-cent tickets for ten dollars, and if we couldn't get a firm promise by the time we'd hopped our feet off it was time to take the ferry back and hit the charpoy. What a life it was, for intelligent young men like us!'

'Innocence,' George said. 'Nothing less.'

'You never went on guard unless you had a bottle of rum. I often found you asleep in the morning. You were on active service, as well. They shot kids like us in the First World War for less than that.'

Racks and drawers went from floor to ceiling along both sides of the narrow shop. Bernard bought vases and bangles, George a chess set, and a box of handkerchiefs whose embroidered ideograms promised health, love and a long life, nonsensical exhortations, since he felt he'd had them already, such was his heightened sense of wellbeing. The proprietor was friendly, their business a spotlight in his dull day. He deplored the new hotels up on the coast, which would have their own shops and so deprive him of custom. Bernard commiserated. The young want sun and sea, discos and sex (a wink for George), but the old-style traveller would always stay in town. The City Lights dance hall had been demolished, the shopkeeper told them, and a hotel put up in its place. Nowadays the water in the Straits was so polluted it wasn't wise to swim there. Things aren't what they were. Bernard praised the man's excellent English, and told him they had served here forty years ago in the army.

He smiled. 'We learned it at school, then. Everything was in English. Now it's not so common.'

'The only thing wrong with the present,' George said, 'is all these motorbikes.' They go around the streets like corpuscles in the bloodstream of the town, few above 125cc, the occasional big 500 swanning along like the king of the road. 'Where do they come from, and where do they go?'

'It's cheap transport,' the proprietor's son said, who had one – the ultimate pollution of people and motorbikes, but progress had to be paid for. And progress was good, they all agreed.

Most of the Oriental Café took up an outside space at the junction of two main roads, the ballet of continually shifting traffic hardly diverting them from the taste of such flavoursome alimentation. Empty shells and crushed claws half hid the plates. George called for another fish, plus rice and a dish of silver beets. 'Five quid each,' said Bernard, 'including the beer. It'll ruin us. Fifty in London, and it wouldn't be half as good.' They were more and more adept with chopsticks. An Indian in jacket and dhoti sitting on a bench apart was putting rice into his mouth with his fingers. 'I can't help feeling that a person goes one step up the ladder of civilization when he takes to chopsticks, or a knife and fork.'

George wondered whether it wasn't a matter only of affluence. 'Those who use implements don't always look civilized, either.'

'Even when we went into the jungle we had a knife, fork and spoon.'

An old Chinese man went by, head and upper part at a sharp angle to his legs, thin white hair and a contented though far-off expression. From his bloodless lips hung a black cigar of the sort George had smoked. He had never forgotten the taste and had craved it ever since, and through it his memory was ineluctably latched to being on guard at the armoury or by the compound gate, in touch with Company

HQ only by the wire of a field telephone. He would craftily extract a packet of such cheroots from his pocket, and pick one carefully out like the choicest of opium stalks. 'Nobody ever found me asleep while on guard. I wouldn't have dared.'

'You were so dopey,' Bernard said, 'you could hardly climb on the gharry to come back for breakfast. It took three of us to haul you up. I put you to bed once, after you fell asleep in the mess. Your head nearly dropped into a bowl of honey.'

George sensed that the Chinese man would lead them to whatever shop sold the cigars, because the one hanging from his lips was halfway smoked but unlit, being guarded as his last. 'You had to be over twenty to stay awake all night.'

'We certainly learned how. Stood us in good stead for afterwards. My first wife appreciated it. Discipline of that sort came in very useful. The longer you sleep the harder it is to wake up. I feel sorry for young kids today.' The life had been easy, slotted into as if he had been brought up to it. Boarded out since a nipper in prep school, the army was just another college where you were taught to kill. He closed the subject off, but it came back. Maybe this doddery old punter they were trailing had been one of the bandits. Or, if he was eighty, he was ancient enough for one of the dead bandits to have been his son. He closed the theme again, snapped it shut, no good regretting what you had lost the power to rectify, and if he hadn't he might have done the same anyway, because the army did not teach you to kill: it taught you to stay alive, so God help anyone who got in your way.

The old man, at a steady pace, led them on. When people moved aside George stayed in his wake, no need to elbow anyone off the pavement or step down. 'It's comforting,' Bernard said, as the man jinked into Kimberley Street, 'that they've kept a lot of the old names.' Campbell, Leith, Gladstone, Light, Dowding, Victoria, Harris, Macalister. 'They don't have a chip on their shoulder about the British like they have in some places.' The old man turned another corner, vibrating as if closer to his quarry. Bernard wished George would follow a geriatric every day. 'It's just the right speed for a stroll.'

Jars of kiddie sweets ('Or perhaps miniature Hash Mixtures,' Bernard suggested) decorated the counter. Inside the shop were cigarettes, a showcase of pipes, and sundry compartments of local cigars against the wall, their cartons gaudy with Chinese ideograms as well as Finest Rangoon Cigars. But Burma was cut off by some loony Marxist regime. 'Trade flourishes in spite of it,' Bernard said, 'and millions of smokes come down the coast by powered junk. The powers that be in Burma want western currency to buy their limousines.'

George pointed to a box of fifty, and the skeletal shop-keeper, bare to the waist, held up four fingers – a quid. Hard to believe, but take it, quick. Discoveries of a lifetime rarely came so cheaply. He split the packet open, took out a short black stump and pulled off the shiny yellow emblem. The first whiff was slightly perfumed.

Bernard stood aside. 'Good?'

Stale bananas, mangrove stench, dead socks and snake dung, an undeniable aroma of oriental tobacco, taste and smell telescoping forty impacted years into one lung-filled moment. 'Perfect.'

'They look ghastly.'

'They are. But they're wonderful. Thought I would never find them.'

'Better you than me.'

George was surprised at saying: 'And better me than anybody.' Surely not? But life had been a snake pit, especially the domestic side. With a good cigar for chemical protection any snake foolish enough to bite would crawl away and die. No fool, he thought himself a somewhat weak and cold person, though on the other hand, and perhaps because of it, he had lived to be sixty, when any stray ambush bullet in the old days could have put paid to him at twenty. In this world only the fresh-cooked were consumed, not the stale, meaning that nobody reached sixty to die of despair. At such an age you at least had a fair chance of a few more years, so with the cigar of youth duly lit, and surrounded by a seemingly benign mist of wellbeing, he walked on down the street.

Bernard positioned himself front-left on the pavement so as to evade the smouldering cloud which George wallowed in because it took him back to where it was not otherwise possible to go. Wouldn't carbolic soap or simple aftershave do just as well? A yearning to return to the primeval slime no doubt existed in everyone, and Bernard also considered himself a victim, otherwise why should he have been snared into such a trip? His talk about Malaya for the last forty years had been a ploy for clinging to youth, yet Jenny had seen it as his enduring desire to come back to the place. Well, he had succumbed, though needed no such compost-heap cigar to re-create the old days now that he was here. He wondered whether recognition would have been more pure and piquant had he been on his own.

You thought about the old days because you were conscious of the difference between then and now. Indeed, you were conscious, which was a blessing. In many instances the difference might not be very much, but then you walked up an open track, the temple complex looming in front as if to fall on you, but now, stalls along the steep approach, selling every kind of tat from fizzy drinks to model pagodas, were so close and joined overhead by matting against the sun that you ascended a tunnel and no longer saw either the buildings or the pristine hills of the central range.

At half past nine the traders were setting out their goods. 'They provide some shade for us at least,' said George, coming up slowly, when Bernard noted the loss of view. 'Not that I don't feel robbed. How can so many people earn a living with so few tourists, though?'

George felt sympathy, because his father had been a shopkeeper, wondered whether such ancestral feeling hadn't something to do with the aching effort of the ascent. He must have forgotten the path was so steep, but suddenly from the tunnel they were on the terrace of the first temple – though too close for the old spectacular view of the agglomeration with its pagoda rearing into the sky – whose recent paint job turned it into a gaudy wedding cake, white and red and gold, blue, green and pink and various day-glo combinations highlighting pinnacles and balustrades, and the main projecting tower which didn't seem high any more because they were seeing it up so close.

Walking through the sun from court to court put a glaze over Bernard's eyes, as if he had seen enough and wanted to flee, or as if he hadn't seen enough because he hadn't yet demolished an idol's face or pulled a piece off the wedding cake. A touch of the sun, George thought, hoping it would pass without a spectacular show.

The statues in the Great Hall of the Buddhas were behind glass, hard to see in the shimmering light. 'They think we might steal the things.' Bernard wiped sweat from cheeks and forehead. 'Or scratch our names on them.'

'In the old days we didn't,' George said. 'So why should we now? Even hooligan swaddies respected art and beauty.' On the floor before the Great Mother a young dark-haired New Zealander unashamedly prostrated herself, oblivious to others, her being permeated with adoration. She wore a dress of coloured stripes – purples, browns and sombre reds – and glanced at a small piece of paper on coming up and going down so as to make the correct incantations.

Bernard brought a handful of joss from one of the monks. 'Might as well light a few for the family – past, present and future.'

'Hopeful, aren't you?'

'I'm not dead, am I?'

A Japanese man planted them in a large golden bowl

of sand, silent prayers between each dip. Bernard deployed his joss with uncharacteristic seriousness, eyes half-closed to recall the face of departed friend or relative. Then with deliberation he planted each one at a slightly different angle in the sand, and lit them so that the group looked like fire-arrows landed from the crackshot archer of a barbaric army.

Forty years ago George had coolly ignored the religious aspect of the temple, but in those days, when thought and action were so wedded that he lived by the moment – or so he supposed – he always knew that in a few months he would be climbing the gangway of a ship that would take him home. He had too much religion as a kid to need more than a vague belief in the Judaic system, which Table of Laws he considered necessary to stop people butchering each other to no good purpose. He looked on such pagan devotions with barely civilized curiosity, though tempered with a vein of respect considering how so many people believed in them.

Walking the halls of laughing big-bellied Buddhas and fearsome warrior gods, he thought that if there was any such thing as God then He must surely have neither shape nor form. He had always liked it that way, yet wondered if after all these years of easy belief he wasn't going back to the more rooted ideas of his father, in no way disturbed that he found such a notion far from depressing.

The half-mile to the Hill Railway – following George's black and white map which, by the grace of sellotape, had survived from the old days – led along a macadamized road, instead of by the previous unpaved track, built up now with villas, shops and schools. The pavement was minimal, and uneven in surface. Being the lowest form of life, pedestrians had to chance their luck against cars and motorbikes that passed by the score.

First in the queue, the rack-and-pinion carriages soon filled, and Bernard decided not to let a woman have his seat, as he once might, because she was about half his age, and would only laugh at such cavalier optimism. A damp breeze cooled them as the train drew itself three thousand feet up through the cutting of the jungle.

Paved tracks radiated from the top station, all unfamiliar, with their well kept dressings of flowered embankments and shrubbed verges. George followed one that had been earthen, between bougainvillaea, cyclamen, hyacinth and jasmine. 'Roses all the way along the straight and narrow primrose path,' said Bernard. They passed the reception area and went through to the shaded verandah of the Starview Hotel.

George felt the first grating of recognition – a bungalow style the same as forty years ago. 'I remember sitting here' – though not very often, he assumed, because hotels like this were beyond their daily stipend. In those days Bernard was the more worldly, southern England born and bred, and knew where such places were before anyone else, barged into them as if he was the new owner. Apart from their common looniness, George read the books that Bernard's father sent, got a taste for talk and life beyond what he had known before.

Bernard called for two bottles of Lion. 'I came up here with Corporal Hollingsworth, to admire the view. All we had was the fare back to Kota Libis. A Chinese man sat at the next table. He wore a good suit, and had rings on his fingers, and we got talking. I forget about what. We were down to our last cent, and he bought us an iced beer each. I'll never forget the taste of that beer. Must be why I like Chinese food. Hollingsworth thought the man was a spy who wanted to pump us for information about our patrols. A real nutter, Hollingsworth was. Touch of the sun, I expect. He probably owns half Liverpool by now.'

The forest, in waves of dark and light green, went downhill and merged with the indistinct band of mainland across the water. 'I wonder what happened to your generous Chinese chap?'

Bernard hooked a finger for the waiter. 'Say he was forty.

Well, he'd be eighty now, wouldn't he? Probably joined his ancestors. Another beer?'

So will we, George mused, in not too long a time, though he knew of no forebears he would especially like to meet. 'There used to be a wooden rail in front of this terrace – instead of a concrete parapet with potted plants along the top.'

Bernard thought for a moment. 'So there was. What a memory.'

A woman from the hotel corridor was asking directions in the trilling and bossy tones of southeast England. 'Probably Surrey,' George said.

'Hampshire. Five dollars on it. If I win, she's mine.'

'Done, you greedy swine.' He remembered seeing her at breakfast, noting that she had changed since then, cool and smart now in a skirt and white manstyle shirt. The English abroad were unpredictable, could be more than normally friendly, or far less so, and George knew that modern ways hadn't entirely made diplomacy obsolete. If she had come from Yorkshire maybe he would have brought her familiarly into the chat, but while he was ruminating on how otherwise to do it Bernard had no qualms: 'It's cooler up here than down below, don't you think?'

'It was a relief to get off that tiny train,' she said.

'Felt like the old rush hour, eh?'

'I wouldn't know.'

George winced when Bernard said at what he thought was too early a moment: 'Why don't you join us, for a drink or whatever? I know we haven't been introduced, but I did set eyes on you at London Airport.'

A smile gave full advantage to her shapely mouth, which she spoiled by placing a cigarette there. 'Did you?'

'You're not easy to forget.'

She laughed. 'I don't know about that' and clattered a chair in coming from two tables along, amused at their standing oh so politely, and even more at Bernard holding out a chair for her.

George beat him in the race to get matches for her cigarette, but a lighter hidden in her palm whisked a flame up before he could strike. 'I think I noticed you at breakfast yesterday.'

'You probably did. I thought you were one of those English people who are too snooty to acknowledge anyone else.'

'And I imagined you didn't want to be bothered.' He decided to shut up, and enjoy the scenery. She smiled, but as if only half agreeing with him. They chatted awhile. 'It's pleasant here,' she said, deciding there was no need to be stand-offish: they seemed harmless and pleasant enough. 'My father often mentioned the place.'

'He knew it?'

'None better. I was reading some of the letters he wrote to my mother. "I went up to the Starview Hotel for tiffin." Only he called it *Starve You*, as a joke, though he said they did anything but that. It took me a whole flight from Heathrow to see through his pun, but it dawned when I noticed Star View in the guidebook. It was his favourite place on the island.'

'I don't think there's a more precious spot anywhere.' Bernard seemed awed by her reminiscence – though George knew better. 'What was your father doing here?'

The two top buttons of her shirt had come undone so that on pushing a hand to her greying hair they had a glimpse of her bra. 'He was the governor of the jail.'

George came straight in, to span what gap her statement might make, though why he should feel any possible guilt on her part as being connected to himself he couldn't think. 'As for us, we were here forty years ago.'

'National service?'

'Oh, a bit before those wallahs,' Bernard said. 'We've come to look the place over. And give our wives and girlfriends a break. What would you care to drink?'

'He must have been here at the same time,' she said.

'I've ordered coffee, thank you. I don't suppose you met him, though, because you were too well behaved, I'm sure.'

'We certainly were,' Bernard laughed, and grated his chair to get closer. 'We're going to have lunch, and we would be honoured if you'd join us.'

George supposed that they had better introduce themselves, and Bernard agreed, covering her indecision by telling their names. 'The place has changed quite a bit,' he added. 'Still recognizable, but it's peculiar coming back, all the same.'

'I've never been here, except as a baby,' she said. 'My father was a prisoner of war with the Japanese, and there wasn't much left of him by the time they'd done. Fortunately my mother was in England, but she didn't recognize him when he came off the aeroplane – well, not for a few minutes. He recovered, pretty much, then he was given his old job back. Not that I think he ever really recovered. And then he got cancer, would you believe it? Anyway, I've come out here to visit a few of the places he mentioned. To see what it was like, I suppose.'

They made a slot of silence out of respect for his memory. 'The three of us seem to be in the same boat,' Bernard said, which George thought a bit all-embracing, though supposed he was only trying to clear away any possible gloom.

Her smiled proved him to be right. 'A sentimental journey, if you like. I don't know why I left it so long, except that it wasn't easy to save money on my salary, with a mortgage and all that. My name's Gloria, by the way. And I'll join you for lunch, though I will pay for my own.'

'We wouldn't hear of it.' Perhaps Bernard wasn't used to dealing with such independence. 'I hope it's not Women's Lib rearing its ugly head!'

'Hardly. It's common sense, and pride. They've been around a long time, wouldn't you say?'

It made little difference either way, George thought, having pulled heavily on his bank account for spending money, fifty pounds a day for this no-stinting, once-in-a-lifetime trip. And nowhere close to that much was flowing from his wallet. He could never have predicted it would be so dirt-cheap.

The small round table was barely enough in size for the various dishes, but George enjoyed being close to her as, so obviously, did Bernard, who managed to face her directly. Such talk was pleasant, even civilizing. He liked the almost bell-like harmony of her southern accent, had always found it attractive in a woman, almost sexually so, and he was happy that she went on talking.

She worked for a solicitor in Guildford, she said, had a garden flat in a house on the outskirts. A neighbour was looking after her dog, a four-year-old bull terrier that let her sleep safe at night – these days. She had always wanted to move closer to London, but had left it too late, prices having gone crazy now. Mostly she went on her holidays to Greece, with a woman friend, because she didn't travel to such places alone. Not that she was ever pestered. She knew how to deal with that sort of thing. But company was always acceptable, especially if you and the person you travelled with knew how to leave each other alone. This time no one had the finances to come with her, and in any case she preferred to do this journey on her own, to get the full effect, as it were, of whatever impressions she might have. But the hope of an intense recall of her father hadn't materialized, at least not so far, though she supposed there might still be time.

'If you think we can help,' George said, 'just let us know.'

It was too early for anything but irony. 'You can be sure I will,' she laughed.

Bernard was quiet, and George felt that his own spell, such as it was, of being back in Malaya, had been disturbed by her talk, though he was pleased with the encounter. She was having trouble with her chopsticks. 'It must be what your father ate,' Bernard said. 'I imagine he liked Chinese food.'

She hesitated, didn't know. He had never really said what he ate. 'He wasn't that kind of person, or so my mother told me. He was very taciturn. His POW experience changed him entirely.' Her rhythm of speech suggested to George that she lived alone, or had for some time. Childless, most likely, divorced five years ago, perhaps. She also thought before she spoke, more than most people anyway, which wasn't much, but you could sense it. This made her both more, and less interesting. More because she might have something to conceal, and less because what she did have to hide might never be discovered. It was wonderful how sharp your faculties became when you had lived for years with a wife who had grown to despise you. Unadulterated love couldn't have done it half so well, at least with someone like him, a conclusion not exactly flattering, though he didn't know what else it was, and hardly worth pondering on since he was here for a break after the confrontation that had thank God ended at last.

'He was a dedicated man,' Gloria said. 'All his life he believed in good order and administration. Never made any money, of course, but then, that wasn't his idea.'

Clouds were coming over. It might even rain. Bloody waffle, George thought. He was a jumped-up prison warder who locked people up and handed out bread and water, or whatever the equivalent had been in this kind of place. And yet, he saw the uncertainty in her eyes, as if she was trying to convince herself of his kindness, and his passion for duty.

'Such people usually do die poor.' Bernard lifted the last fat prawn out of its sauce. 'It's the way of the world.'

This pleased her. 'Well, not poor exactly. My mother managed on his pension, though she only lived five years after his death. So at eight I was sent from Weston-super-Mare to be brought up by her sister in Guildford. I hesitate to call her aunt. She was a complete stranger, and had lived on her own till then. She had very funny ways.'

'The War ruined a lot of people.' Bernard's avuncular

touch of her hand was merely a movement to divert her from the embarrassment that, to judge by her sudden flush, such talk had lured her into.

'Not everyone.' George saw the War as having improved his life by prising him away from the spiritual restrictions of the north of England. 'I've talked about myself,' she said, 'but what about you two?'

'Dull professional men. I organize the dissemination and selling of books, that kind of thing, though I suppose it could just as well be cigarettes. I even did that at one time. George here was a schoolteacher, the sort who ruined kids in the sixties by letting them do their own thing.'

'If we hadn't relaxed the curriculum a bit they would have taken things into their own hands. It was the times we lived in.'

'They need maths, science and languages,' Bernard said, 'not play acting and art and sociology. You can hardly get a youngster into the office these days who can spell and do arithmetic. It's a disgrace.'

The big peak on the mainland was entirely covered. A whiff of coolish wind moved leaves in the plant pots. George thought it a bit below the belt to reactivate their old argument before a stranger. 'Try teaching the sort of kids I had to deal with maths and science. They'd laugh at you. It was a matter of keeping sixteen-year-old roughnecks as tall as yourself under control. In the old days they were in factories from fourteen.'

'I suppose the children did enjoy it, though.' She smiled directly at him, showing her beautiful mouth.

'And indeed still do,' Bernard said pompously. Bored with what he had let loose, he turned to her. 'We thought of walking back. Do you want to try it?'

Her eyebrows formed the question. 'Won't it be too much in this heat?'

George certainly thought so. Three thousand feet down through the forest was no joke.

'Not for a couple of old jungle bashers like us,' Bernard said. 'What say you, George?'

The map was uncontoured, schematic, but they had only to choose a track that kept descending. George spoke from the cloud of his black cheroot. 'I'm game.'

'I'll give it a try, then,' she said, 'after we've split the bill three ways.'

The paved track, too recent to be a hairline on George's map, was wide enough for two, but Bernard who walked with Gloria soon couldn't think of anything to say. She didn't care, not expecting entertainment as well as company, interested enough merely to fall in with them for an hour or two.

George took the lead, and chose the left fork when the path divided, as if familiar with the way into the forest of his youth and dreams, down from the white-fronted classical villas on the crests, most of them locked up out of season, and descending into the fecund gloom of a re-entrant.

Gloria came up with him, and after walking for a while said: 'How old are you?'

'Sixty.'

'I'd never have thought it.'

'We both are – just.'

'You seem about forty or fifty.'

'That's kind of you.' His springing step proved that having kept up with sixteen-year-olds hadn't been wasted.

She seemed out of breath. 'We're going at a great rate.'

'It's downhill, luckily.'

'Oh, I don't mind it.'

'That's all right, then.'

She shook a stone from her sandal. 'Who had the idea for this trip?'

'Bernard's wife. He talked so much about the place, for so many years, that she finally packed him off to see it again. Happily, she lumped me in to keep him company.

I'm divorced, just retired, and live on my own, so I was in no position to turn the notion down.'

The walk was resumed, and he hoped Bernard wouldn't catch up too soon. 'You don't seem to have anything in common,' she said.

They'd certainly had plenty at one time, and if what they still had was apparently superficial it could be even more profound because of that. 'He's a great friend. Very open and generous. I've never had one for so long.'

Poor you, she thought, imagining therefore that like her he hadn't had many. 'It's often that way with opposites.'

'Once upon a time we were similar in our lunacies. We still are, on a certain level.'

'I suppose this is what they call the jungle,' she remarked, as the path steepened, twisting between giant trees laced with creepers.

'You could say that. Forty years ago there were few paths, and I got lost here a couple of times. I once came to a cliff face, and didn't know how to get down. But I did. Getting lost soon teaches you how to find your way about.'

She fell behind, but it was restful being alone, no one visible on the track. All the same, she felt annoyed at being left on her own, scared almost that something – she couldn't imagine what, which didn't help – might come at her from behind the trees. Heels scraped and her insteps ached, but she kept up a speed as if gliding down, heart drumming at the gradient. She paused, for breath and to hear the uncanny voice of the forest, strange squawks as from monkeys, the belligerent twitter of birds, a decayed branch dropping into dry leaves – no human or mechanical noises to disturb, the nearest airconditioned hotel a long way off.

George went on, sweating copiously from the beer and food at lunch. Undergrowth fell steeply to the giant tree boles in an overgrown gully, and he was drawn towards going there. Concealed by foliage, he would crash through,

93

and find his way, even if it took far longer, and exhaustion spent him out. The temptation was vibrant, but the will void. The impossibility of doing what he had once so thoughtlessly performed smote him to embarrassment. A sudden fear stopped him plummeting through the concealing bushes, but fear of what, he couldn't say. To get bitten by a snake was most unlikely. They fled, poor creatures, well in advance of footsteps, although he had known someone stung by an ill-tempered viper in the Pyrenees. In the old times he had never considered such perils. Nowadays loneliness and the dark were greater plagues, but even they were harmless. The barrier between this unevenly paved track and a plunge through the brushwood back to the nearest kampong was so impossible to push aside, though composed of nothing but air, that he could only laugh and go on his way, knowing that the time had gone when he could go down into the forest and succumb to the luxury of the dark.

'You're setting us a fair lick,' Bernard said. 'I thought I'd catch up, but I'm sweating like a drunkard. A bowser of booze would be a godsend.'

'Drawn by a bloke on a bike.' George was also drenched, not worth remarking, but so puffed that he stopped. The cool hilltops were well behind, the wooded gully warm and stifling. 'I'd lay down under the tap.' Stupidity inconceivable that he hadn't thought to bring his old webbing-covered water bottle. Salt tablets and copious amounts of water were the order of the day. 'How did you get on with Gloria?'

'Frigid as a fish,' Bernard said, 'I shouldn't wonder.' She walked into view, steady and upright, shoulderbag hanging, her wave a very quirky kind of signal.

'We'll wait,' George said.

Being on her own had brought peace, no real fears in a place like this. But just as she had got used to it she found them waiting for her. 'Now I know why my father loved the place,' she said. 'It's so beautiful here in the forest, much better than up among the villas.' Her shirt was pasted to the upper part of her chest with sweat, emphasizing a shapely bosom. She hadn't had children, George surmised, whether or not she had been married. He was pleased at his curiosity, a lightening of the spirit. The last stages of his marriage had been so fraught that he had been interested in no woman beyond its anguished boundaries.

Bernard, rare for him, was less than kind: 'It's a hell of a long way down, beautiful or not.' Then he checked his tone. 'The first time I saw it I thought the same. Youth is wonderful, full of true feelings.'

Reconciled, they walked in a group, only the slap of feet audible, and hard breathing from the effort of a descent which seemed to go on forever. The track was blocked by a landslip, and Bernard offered to help her over trunks and broken roots.

'It's all right. I can manage.' But she lurched, so thought what the hell? and took his hand to scramble the last few rocks into the clear.

The clammy heat weighed a ton, amazing how much liquid one could lose. Bernard, having mastered his own pace, was in front and out of sight. 'I hope I didn't offend him,' she said to George.

'Certainly not. He's a good sort.'

Try never to offend anyone, her aunt had often said. It costs nothing to be polite. Unless someone is offensive to *you*, of course, but that's quite rare. 'I can see that.'

'Generous to a fault.'

'You're very loyal.'

He caught her sarcasm. 'Next to godliness, isn't it, loyalty?'

The concept seemed to worry her. 'Why not?'

'Are you married?' he asked.

'Not likely. Life's far too interesting, don't you think?'

'I was married for over thirty years, so I have to agree.'

'At least you've thought about it.'

'That's about all that's left to you after a while.'

'You're a cynic, really.'

'A realist, let's say.' He felt pompous, a label – among others – that his wife often put on him.

When she went on holiday her expectation of some kind of emotional adventure occasionally led her into an attachment with a woman – when no suitable man was available. She certainly didn't know about this one, but surprised herself by saying: 'I usually find that the best men are married.'

And without thinking he replied: 'It often seems to me that all the best women are single. Married women are soon ruined by their husbands, or spoiled by husbands who aren't able to make them happy.'

'Who can make anyone happy?'

Well, he thought, bringing back an old phrase, there may be no flies on her, but there are marks where they've been. 'Two people in love can make each other happy.'

She was impressed by his wisdom, yet wondered at the implied familiarity, which was more subtle than his friend's, and for that reason to be parried, though with a smile. 'I'm glad I never married a person like you.'

He found it a gentle blow compared to some, and in such a landscape, but he would say nothing further on the only subject at which he considered himself an expert, glad when they caught up with Bernard. 'If I had my barometer I could tell us how high we were.'

Bernard sat with his legs stretched along a fallen tree trunk. 'I'll bet you were popular with the kids, with all your little bits of knowledge.'

'I took parties to the Pyrenees, trekking,' he said to Gloria.

'It must have been fun with such a guide.' She opened a clean handkerchief to wipe her lips. 'Thought I heard a car.'

'We can't have more than a thousand feet left to go,' Bernard said.

George guessed they were barely halfway. ' "*Chi va piano va sano; chi va sano va lontano*," ' he quoted, in case they were in a hurry to be going. To the side of the track, on the minor growth of a re-entrant, was a plank table under a palmleaf shelter, a resting place with benches, and one after the other they came to it, nothing to say till breathing was calm and leg muscles rested.

'In my experience,' Bernard said, 'it's worse going down than coming up.' He turned to Gloria. 'Are you all right, though?'

'All we have to do is keep putting one foot in front of the other,' she said, 'eh, George?'

He was startled at his name from her lips, though not flattered by the inflexion. Bernard had broached the trek, and she had come in on the idea. 'We've got all the afternoon. There's no hurry.'

'I want to get it over.' Bernard stood up, the trudgery no longer enjoyable. 'So I'll put in another few yards, if you'll excuse me.' He walked jauntily till hidden by a bend, but then they caught up and soon left him behind.

'Are you really all right?'

'Never felt better,' she said. 'I walk a lot at home, as well as play tennis. It's your friend I'm concerned about.'

George smiled at the amount of worrying that went on when they had only just met. The track descended at a gradient painful to the soles, the gully widening to let sunlight through, fomenting dampness that gave steam to breathe instead of air. 'When I was twenty this sort of thing wasn't any easier than it is now. I had more sense than to walk the whole way from top to bottom, though. When you're young you're far too wise to waste energy. Only the old are foolish enough to chew off too much.' I must stop bumbling – but he couldn't, didn't see why he should. In any case, she seemed to be listening. 'We lazed around much of the time, except for an occasional run up into the jungle after terrorists – or bandits, as we called them then.'

Maybe he had something to talk about, after all. 'And did you find any?'

'One or two.' A shiver returned from the zone of when

they did, that little grey vignette of a complete orb-eyeball on a man's chest, bloody threads attached, blown from a head mushed by half a Sten gun magazine. The shade of guilt that had periodically returned was again brushed aside, and he didn't want to talk about that. 'In camp we would go for a swim, or a row in the Straits, but we always knew when we were getting tired and ought to go back.' Specks of blackness danced before his eyes, and a pause reinforced his point.

'Yet it's the young who die,' she said, the implication clear that George had known how to survive, and might not be making too good a job of it now.

She was censorious, but how could he say what tribulations had brought her to it? 'I'm sixty,' he said, 'but I've never felt older than twenty-five. Which comes of having taught young people most of my life. Or maybe that's how I am.' He wasn't far enough out of marriage to decide whether she looked on him with pity or contempt. 'You go on down. I'll come in a bit. It's not often I'm alone in a place like this.'

She wasn't listening, liked her curiosity to be satisfied in small doses, a lifetime devotee, she decided with amusement, of homeopathic effects. 'I thought I saw a guinea fowl. Or something moved.'

He followed her to the edge of the road. 'The jungle's full of life, quite beyond us to see it, of course.'

He was only perceptive about things long gone, because he had had time to mull on them, seemed not in tune with the moment. They were alone in the forest, the air warm and damp as if about to generate lightning. He wouldn't dare, she decided, and even less would she, though the moment and the place seemed natural. 'I'm surprised you were a teacher.'

Her face was a few inches away, those bow lips, a mole on her left cheek, and deep grey almost lifeless eyes. She stood, an arm across her chest, legs apart, face at an enquiring tilt. The pores of her skin, all of her warm perspiring body was drawing him, yet what if his senses were inexact? For the rest of his life he would regret not kissing her, but could no more do so than plunge into the declivity and make his way through the forest to civilization.

They moved away, and he knew he should be craving to die, but an earthlike optimism held him above such solutions. 'Nothing else I could be except a teacher,' he said. 'What would you expect?'

She shrugged, unsatisfied with his remark, tried to keep any petulance out of her tone, but didn't manage it. 'I wouldn't know, would I?' But in the forest she felt she could ask anything. 'Was your marriage a happy one?'

His laugh was genuine, admitting inextricable thought, but wondering why he had let himself in for this. A pair of iridescent dragonflies helicoptered into the gully. 'You want the truth? I wouldn't mind it myself. Everything's true concerning a marriage. Or equally false.'

'You do seem to want it both ways.'

'Well, your question was rather a funny one.' He had the sense of talking to a much younger woman, which indeed she was. 'But I don't suppose it's any funnier than my attempt to answer would be.'

She walked away, turned the bend in front, giving him up to the torment of his confusions, but also to the solace of being alone. An engine was working somewhere, its heavy beat coming from a place below, then moving as if from above or behind. Bernard had probably gone through the bush to meet them at the bottom, the untapped strength of his old looniness carrying him any distance.

He wanted to catch up and walk with her, feel her close though not speak, but regulated his steps so as to stay clear, troubled by the sound of the machine which, neither an aeroplane raving for lift-off at the airport, nor a boat beating a homeward track towards the harbour, filled the forest on all sides with noise. If she reached the bottom of the hill first, caught a taxi to town, and he didn't see her again, he would take a memory from Malaya that would haunt him, which was strange, because he wasn't so young or so plain daft as to fall in love.

The idea of cutting off into the thicket on a compass course so as to get to the main road before her did not seem outlandish, but he maintained his pace, unable to deviate, because only actions ostensibly without thought had any meaning. Fate, or whatever it was, had ambushed him on every corner of his life's road, and he could not think that anything other than fate would decide for him now. Which makes me, as my wife often said, lazy and indecisive.

The noise of machinery seemed to break from every globule of sweat, shook leaves, made trees reverberate. She waited halfway along the next stretch, glad at not being strange to strenuous walking, for she belonged to a group which rambled once a month in Sussex or Hampshire, but even so, the heat in this place tapped too much energy.

'Rest every couple of hundred yards,' he said, 'like me. We used to haul ourselves up instead of down, and carry a heavy pack. But we had frequent breaks.'

She was fatigued with him as well, as if she had known him too long already. 'What's that awful machine noise?'

He was glad not only he heard it. 'Seems to be getting closer.'

They could only stand and wait for its apparition, a roaring machine hunger eating up everything as it descended, trampling all in its track. A giant yellow earth mover, with a lowered scoop of shining steel, came around the bend, collecting stones or brush that had fallen down the slopes. Diesel smoke fluted from a yellow chimney, pistons ready to lower the scoop, or the driver with wheel and levers to slew it in any direction. Gridded headlamps bracketed his position, tyre treads that would obscure a hand cleaning them out.

A young man in wire-rimmed spectacles, with a drooping moustache and short black hair waved from high under his canopy. Bernard's arm gripped one of the uprights, the white licence numbers immediately below his chest holding him in a convict mugshot, his shout inaudible above the engine grind.

George and Gloria stood to let it pass, but the driver stopped his engine, noise still vibrating their ears. 'What are you two doing on shanks's pony?' Bernard called from on high. 'It's a lot better like this.'

'Climb up,' the driver said. 'All are welcome. There is a long way to go yet.' He took out a pack of cigarettes, lit one in case they needed time to think about it.

'You'll have to hang on, though,' Bernard said. 'It's bloody dangerous.'

She was pretty well done for, thighs turning to stone, throat as if coated with dry blotting paper. 'Let's try.'

Bernard hauled and George stood behind lest she drop back, a glimpse of muscular shapely legs, and a pleasing view of her blue pants. They packed themselves around the driver. 'I once took twenty men down,' he said. 'All standing in the scoop. I didn't lose any of them. A lorry had stalled, you see, trying to get up the hill.'

Hot pistons broke into action and, at the release of the lever, the vehicle charged over potholes and dips as if the ground was shifting under them. 'Track was built ten years ago,' the driver shouted. 'It took two and one half years to finish. I know every bump, like the back of my hand.' He chatted on, hard to hear, forty years old, he said, and had ten children, for which feat Bernard congratulated him.

'It's very good for me,' the man said. 'All of them are in school now.'

At ten miles an hour George's hand was slippy at the rail, needing all strength to maintain a grip as the machine bucked and turned. They couldn't talk, with so much noise, and the effort of staying on, perilously high above the track. If any fell it was a matter of go one and go all, manglement spectacular and maybe fatal. Pale Gloria locked an arm onto his waist, having trust enough in him, the grip comforting, but legs forward all the same and braced by her own strength against the steel plate. A blandfaced grey monkey stared from the roadside. How Scrab would chase them, she thought, smiling to herself.

'Getting close to the village now,' the man said. 'Any minute, and it will appear.' He swung his vehicle along with panache, muscling around frequent bends as if driving a block of flats. Vegetation drew back into a quarry area, sheds in the middle, a row of lorries and fuel tanks at the edge of level ground. A Tamil watchman came out of his palmleaf shade to open the gate across the track. Bernard made the driver happy by handing him a five-dollar bill to buy sweets for his children.

A bus stop and a few thatched houses stood where the public road began. At a stall of green coconuts a workman was sucking out liquid with a straw. George stretched his arms, blood needling back to his fingertips. 'A whole one would be too much for me.' He held it like a football towards Bernard, but he preferred a tin of orange. The stallkeeper lopped the top off with his panga, and made a small hole.

Gloria pushed in a straw. 'I'll share it with you.'

Their foreheads were close, mouths welling up the cool of the strength-giving milk, a taste slightly metallic. George resisted laughing at a strand of her hair passing against him, their cheeks sunk with drinking, as if in a race to get the most. Bernard in looking was no doubt as bemused as he was himself, sucking at the same great pap with Gloria until the two ends of straw in the dark struck air and made a bubbling noise at which they laughed, Gloria blushing though he didn't see why she should.

Eyes down, milk finished, she was meeting him in the dark, the tips of their straws touching. The stallholder chopped the hulk open and gave them spoons to scoop out the pale sloppy flesh.

six

There were sufficient crows in the world for everyone to
have his or her own *doppelgänger* while they continued with
their seemingly unconscious lives. 'Hard to know which one
is mine, though,' Bernard remarked.

A dark-backed, wicked-looking specimen with a nicotine-
stained neck picked a self-assured way along the parapet.
Nevertheless, there was something gracious about the crow,
George decided. 'Very neat and sanitary is the crow, the
cleaner and gleaner.'

'We should thin out their ranks a bit,' Bernard said.
'They're a damned nuisance.' One, poised by the edge of
the pool, eyed their plate of toast. 'A two-two rifle, or even
an airgun, and we would amuse ourselves for days now that
there aren't any bandits.' Functional, intelligent, and maybe
beautiful to each other, to Bernard their ugly voices mocked
the pleasure of music that mankind had nurtured for centu-
ries. 'They're sure to inherit the earth, meanwhile preying
off us with malice and amusement.'

George sighted his pocket compass along the opposite
shore, laid out a bearing on the map, and aimed the binoculars at a pinkish unfinished building of two or three storeys
which could serve as a landmark when they crossed over in
a few days.

The camp must have been towards the end of the sandy

stretch, because a long hut set at an angle to the water seemed a surviving part of it. Huts around the building resembled a holiday camp, and could be where they had erected their tents under the trees forty years ago, so that again he saw the orderly room, company HQ, signals area, cookhouse and billets.

Sharp images faded, and refocusing dissolved all sense of the locality he had fixed on with such certainty. Gloria had gone on her own, tired of them, or of him – or of herself maybe, in which case it was even more necessary for her to be alone. Hard to know which, couldn't guess. Analyse people too much and you never get to know them.

Bernard was reading the *Straits Times*. 'Listen to this. "The Morality Police, in their helicopter yesterday evening, apprehended a woman on the beach north of Muong City because she had been sighted in a compromising position with a man. The man escaped. Further enquiri   are proceeding." '

'Impossible,' George said.

'It's here, in black and white.'

'It's not there at all.'

'I've just read it to you.'

'I know. Disgusting, really. "Spot the cock" must be their favourite game. But I'm talking about the camp where we once roistered after coming back from our patrols.'

'I leave the navigation to you. It's Morality with a capital M, and no mistake. I don't know how the Chinese tolerate it.'

'It's a Moslem country.' George levelled his glasses again. 'I expect they'll make their voices heard if it gets too much.'

'They damn-well ought to. Impossible to imagine them putting up with too much Fundamentalist crap.'

'Now don't get racist – though I have to agree.'

'Racist? Me?' Bernard snapped the paper down. 'I've never had a racist thought in my life. I just hate pompous, self-satisfied, persecuting bigots.'

George recalled a game he had set the children to play in

school when teaching the English Civil War. On their own knowledge of themselves he got them to divide into Cavaliers for King or Roundheads for Cromwell. He imagined Bernard would fit nicely into the former, while he thought he would go for Cromwell, though far from feeling himself a bigot.

A reworking of the bearing told him that the camp would be as much as a quarter of a mile further north, kampongs along that stretch like beads on a string. The needle shivered towards a low yellow building with a reddish roof, so could it be there or, the truth was, it could be any bloody where, but where, he wondered, was Gloria? Easy to imagine how Bernard would laugh if he guessed the turmoil of his speculations.

Bernard folded the newspaper. 'I suppose that's why the City Lights dance hall no longer operates. Too much for the fun-hating Fundamentalists to stomach. I was quite looking forward to another bash with a dusky Eurasian beauty.' A powered canoe with an old man and his daughter, or maybe his wife, or even his girlfriend, Bernard thought, was smacking along through greenish water, heading for the main pier. The woman was rowing, the prow almost under every time the tiny wooden dugout lurched forward. He wondered about their lives. Who were they? What living did they make? Why were they going where they were going? Impossible to know. You couldn't get into the skin and into the spirit of anyone else just by looking. Even decades of shared existence didn't always help, so why bother?

George considered it too hot to get a book from his room, watched nimbus clouds swing into view over the high peak, similar heads hovering where he thought the old camp to be. Otherwise the sky was blue, hazy where it met the trees. A quartet of young girls splashed in the pool, talking and laughing their little secrets, breasts bobbing up and down in flowered swimsuits when they jumped to avoid a boy who bombed among them. Gloria's probably wangled an introduction to get inside the prison where daddy used to work. Peculiar of her to latch so much on him at her age. He had hardly thought of his own father since he died. Didn't even see her at breakfast.

'Why don't we go and look at the Butterfly Farm on the northern coast?' he said. Hard to say what he hadn't taken an interest in. Those bloody kids had obliged him to study everything, including lepidoptera. 'We'll pack our swimsuits as well, in case we see a nice place for a splash. On the way we can look in at Fort Perth, where we used to spend our leaves.'

There was no such place on the map, but the Indian taxi driver said it was a divisional headquarters of the Malaysian Army these days, so didn't think they would be able to get in for a quick look. In any case, it had been much altered, though the trees over the beach were still there. 'As, no doubt,' said Bernard, 'are the boulders we used to sit on contemplating our navels between one meal and the next.'

For some way out of town the highrise suburbs distorted all views. Not much was familiar, as if the pockets of the mind had been picked by the thief of time. George wondered whether he hadn't lived too long, in coming back to search for what no longer existed. He craved a Golden Age, without changes, the past to be always in the present, and the present never any different from what had long since gone, such timeless paradises as had never existed in countries where progress had been delineated by the bully of history. That the present should be so cut off from the past was uncivilized, no matter what gew-gaws progress pushed into our throats. Technical accomplishments should have stopped at the wireless and the bicycle.

'Progress is wonderful, though,' dear old sybaritic Bernard responded. 'I love my BMW and Super Hifi Compact Disc player. And as for coming here by jet in fourteen hours instead of taking a month on a steamship, and being cossetted by those lovely young ladies, well, far be it from me to whinge, as the Aussies say.'

George's opinions were flawed, and he knew it. In England things also changed, so why should he want to stop the clock for Malaysia? He hadn't noticed such movement in England because he lived there, but anyone who had been away forty years would have seen that the place had also altered entirely, and no doubt for the better, as times had improved things in Malaya. He had wanted the impossible for as long as he could remember, even as a young soldier of twenty gazing at the camp on the mainland and knowing exactly where it was, yet knowing almost nothing else about either himself or the world. But what he knew now, which he could not have known then, was that in those days he had known more than he realized, and he had also known far more than the George at this moment, because of the distance in time and place between the two utterly different people. The person of forty years ago had died somewhere along the way in order that he, the present George, might get newly born and properly live, something which he had never been able to accomplish. And believing in all the formalities, he had come back to bury him.

Each tree-bordered bay and half moon of sand was much like another, palm trees bending over rocks and water. 'As in the old days,' Bernard said, 'when we had whole beaches to ourselves.'

'In two months the Australians come,' the driver called out. 'Then it's different. Much more work for me.' He stopped at Fort Perth. 'Now you can take photographs, for old time's sake.'

'They'll think we're snapping military installations,' George said.

The driver laughed. 'It's all right just for one minute. Nobody will see. I wait till you finish.'

'I don't fancy going back to England with a bullet up my arse.' A bulled-up and blancoed sentry, his beret at a raffish slant, stood inside the gate. 'He's looking very suspicious and nasty.'

'Let's chance it.' Bernard thought back to the Emergency, when a squad of the Malay Regiment caught asleep in a hut beyond the airstrip they were supposed to guard were drummed out of the service and sent back to their villages. It seemed a different army now.

'Perhaps it's best not to tangle with them,' George said. 'They're a bit touchy these days, I'll bet.'

Bernard had hoped to stand on the beach, and walk to the gun emplacement on the headland where they had taken each others' photographs, wearing tailormade drill of almost phosphorous white. Why otherwise had he come to see the old place? The taxi beckoned like a hearse. He felt dead, expedition phut, spirit gone. After forty years it was like seeing a film in Technicolor, a soulless remake of the original faded classic of black and white. He got back in the car. 'I expect you're right.'

Gloria came along the winding path. The natural habitat of the Butterfly Farm was roofed by green mesh to hold in the huge black and orange, blue and russet specimens. Some fluttered through the steam heat with a chrysalis attached like torpedoes to their underbellies, or flattened against the mesh as if trying to escape to proper jungle beyond.

'Who can blame them?' said Bernard. 'We didn't see any on our descent from the hill. Must all be in here, poor things. Not that there isn't plenty of space for them to feel free, though if they were flying about outside they'd soon be captured by greedy fingers and sold to this place for a bob or two.' Nevertheless, he thought it better for them to chance it. 'Oh for the old kukri to slit the canopy and let them go.'

'Such days of madness are over for us,' George said. 'Nor do I think the owners would appreciate it. We'd be in a labour battalion building a dam or a new airport before we could turn round. It would hardly find favour with the tourists, either. Look how they enjoy staring at the specimens in this lepidopterical zoo.'

She felt the darkness under her eyes, had noticed in the mirror that age was showing, such signs only useful in what they were hiding. 'I thought it was you two. I could tell your voices anywhere, chatting merrily away. I never expected to bump into you here.'

I suppose it had to be somewhere, said George's look, as if he had put back a bottle of whisky and not yet slept it off. Must be the heat, he thought. I suppose we got used to it all those years ago.

'I did hope we hadn't seen the last of you,' Bernard said, ever gallant, at the post before slow George.

She looked into a den of giant millipedes. 'I wouldn't like them running up my arm. Not sure why I came here, really.' She moved her bag to the other shoulder. The stick insects were hard to see, until they moved, everything in the place so blending with nature. 'I hate creepy-crawlies.'

'Not more than they hate us.' It was the custom to throw coins into the scorpion pit, the place, George smiled, where dreams undoubtedly come from. 'Did that long walk down the hill tire you out?'

Bernard walked off over a humpbacked wooden bridge to search for the Rajah Brooke. 'I wouldn't have missed it for anything,' she said. 'But I lay on the beach yesterday, pampering myself in the sun.'

'We weren't up to much, either. How is your recollection of things past?'

'I think I'll forget about all that. It's only a holiday, really.' She sounded disappointed, and he thought he could understand why. An Englishman and his wife, whose accents told him they came from Yorkshire, beamed high-price Japanese equipment onto every specimen. One huge butterfly after another came to rest on the salty sweat of the man's arm, from hairy wrist up to the elbow, so that he looked like a looter from a Swiss city with his swag of original watches. They sucked happily, and he smiled as if he had made friends for life, while his wife took one careful shot after another.

'Have you been to have a look at the prison yet?' They walked slowly, as if afraid to tread on a butterfly.

'I've rather gone off the idea. What about you, and your old places?'

'Can't even find them. A mischievous scene shifter pulls them out of the way when we trouble to look. They've obliterated the past so much since Independence that the atmosphere's gone from whatever we might have remembered. Still, we'll be off to the mainland soon, to find the place where we once set out into the jungle, which is all we came for, really.'

The exit from the Farm led through a shopping compound of stalls and tables exhibiting gimcrack mementoes at all prices, so there was no excuse for not buying something. Bernard chose a couple of large framed butterflies. 'I'll tell them at the office I shot 'em from the back of the sultan's elephant.'

'Another exploit of Butterfly Bill,' George said. 'But don't forget to mention my part in their demise.'

'You were one of the beaters.'

Gloria shrugged, her rather square shoulders turning for her to sift through a packet of trinkets. Bernard held up a large red warlord's flag straight off the loom, all flowers and dragons. 'It's just the dressing gown to take when I go away for the weekend. I'd better get one for Jenny as well. She's about your size, George. See if this fits.'

Why not? Gloria glanced, and he noticed. He liked to think he took in everything, while those around thought that he didn't, an aggressive anonymity which occasionally protected him. If he opted out of trying the damned thing on she might begin to wonder, but if she went far in that direction she wouldn't be more wrong. He patted himself. 'She's got a bit more up here than I have.'

'Never mind. It's loose enough. She'll be delighted to have proof of my infinite regard.'

George was glad that he was no longer the target of her smile, a fact which signified too much for him to feel comfort, her smiles being the sort that divided her from others rather than expressing delight. Not that he was old, but even though she was not young there was a variation in their ages that made him uneasy at whatever might be in her mind. Nor was it a difference of sex, as Bernard would have suggested. In looking on them with something close to affectionate contempt she was doing neither them nor herself justice, seemed in fact so much in the grip of her uncertainties that he wondered about the wisdom of getting to know her – supposing he was given half the chance. If there was no such thing in her mind, why was he thinking about her? He had too recently disembarrassed himself of that state of tension to enter it carelessly again.

Outside, they immediately sought shade. She only wanted to swim, but on the beach yesterday she had been pestered, and forced to leave. So she would stay with them, and make the suggestion, shaming though it was to need chaperones.

'A wonderful idea,' Bernard said. 'Maybe we'll get a drink, as well.'

George wanted a siesta, to shut off his thoughts, like a man suffering from permanent exhaustion. After thirty-odd years of marriage he had ended up (or had he? he wondered) in a furnished room – flowered wallpaper, a settee and an armchair, a desk in one corner and a small square table in the other, narrow bookcase up to the ceiling. The kitchen was a mere cupboard for pots, a stove and a sink. From the window he could look into the greenery of a back garden, perfect for a man alone, a devastation of the spirit but at least he could call it peace and stay sane. Meanwhile he was attempting to connect with this livid Malayan landscape, and overprint it onto a past that had been so short it might never have existed. Yet it was sharply detailed nevertheless, a not entirely useless exercise, because he had never felt more fit and free than in trying to remember it.

They walked through the nearest hotel to a long stretch of sand, and undressed surreptitiously, as if the morality police might be spying from overhead. In the old days loin-clothed Malayan fishermen rowed their praus from the stand-up position, speeding towards acres of fishing traps sticking out of the water. 'It's polluted nowadays,' George said. 'No fish any more.' The mainland was a length of shadow lined with palms, and the only way to find the camp would be to walk a couple of miles along the road from Kota Libis.

'But who,' Bernard said, 'could schlepp so far in this steam pudding heat?' He splashed in, calling only to Gloria: 'Aren't you coming?'

George's cheroot smoked invisibly in the heat. Cameras, spectacles, watches, passports and travellers cheques would be a golden handgrab for anyone nipping from behind the trees. 'I'll watch your belongings, and be in later.'

'Good thinking,' she smiled. 'Shan't be long.'

The brazen sun was absorbed by overcast, a pleasant climate when accustomed to it, though he put on his straw hat so that his brains wouldn't fry in their pan. Bernard swam strongly, going far out. Look after him, Jenny said, he's precious to me. And so he would, with his life, he supposed, but what if he was nipped by a watersnake, or squeezed by a dose of the cramp and went under before anyone could get to him?

He disappeared, came up in a different place, porpoised around. Then he was cleaving the slight swell on his way inshore. Gloria did a circle, trod water within her depth, nothing between her eyelids, and an infinity of blue when she lay on her back, no dreams any more, life for the moment wonderful.

George walked down the slope. 'What's it like?'

'A bit warm and sludgy.' She stood in the shallows,

adjusted the bathing suit around her breasts. 'But it's refreshing.'

He released himself into a crawl, the water a velvet waistcoat till he scraped his knees on a rock. Bernard came weltering by in a cloud of spray, unconscious of the passing. Sky was dark across the Straits, and George wondered what distance he would make if he went on till power failed. To divide it by half and get the radius of action was something he had never been able to calculate, so it was guesswork all the way, which took him far enough nonetheless.

He swung round to see a wild swaying of palm heads signalling that it was time to get in. Troughs opened under his chest, and he tried to keep the beach in sight instead of being swung to unwelcome views of open water, but the sea was a bad playmate, and pulled him by the legs into a trough, so that he couldn't then get over the summit.

He pushed as if against the base of a wall to prevent being drawn backwards, present and past about to merge into a last unshakeable sensation, no more arguing to do, and he enjoyed the perverse effort of keeping them close, as well as the help which the storm seemed to give, knowing (and this was not unpleasant, either) that his father all through life had assumed the only truth to be that the present and the past were indivisible, the one sure belief that had kept him to his Bible, and pegged him against the board of reality.

Trees shook as if to scatter their palm fronds. He cursed at the bile of saltwater, played a torpedo at the crawl, then jacked with his feet again and again towards the shallows, an arm and a hand scooping at the vast amount in front as if to fill a desert behind.

He would drive to exhaustion, then relax his muscles in the buoyancy of amniotic fluid, yet taking no chances. Understanding his father so late in life alarmed him more than the rabid water. Surrender to forces he had always hated filled him with an anger he could hardly afford in this situation, as if by not having realized such a truth sufficiently early to put it through the testing incinerator of thought he had wasted his life.

It was a neglect that made him go through life with two of him instead of one, and it must have been the least familiar side that had got him to the age of sixty, the one which would not allow him to go under and forced him to accept such a revelation.

What felt like gravel at his face was the gunning of rain, a violent sandpaper downpour pitting the water all around, scouring the beach and the trees. The effort so warmed him that he did not much care whether or not he reached the shore, but suddenly he felt sand, and got to his feet.

'Thought we'd lost you,' Bernard said. They walked onto the terrace of the hotel. 'We kept your togs dry, though.'

She ordered orange juice for them. 'He was about to come out for you.'

'I certainly wasn't. We had a grandstand view of your heroic struggle. Didn't you hear us cheering as you fought for your life?'

They enjoyed a bit of friendly chaff, but he knew Bernard would have helped had the need been real. Which it almost was, his tambourine heart only now settling back to its usual pace. Gloria saw them as irresponsible nitwits, because by not acknowledging any peril that hit them they risked becoming its victims. Making believe danger didn't exist was only slightly less irresponsible, and angered her as much. Apart, she didn't doubt that they acted their age and behaved properly, but together they ceased to be normal beings. So many people were like them it was no wonder that the country was in such a state. Most men had no genuine attachment to the career they had stumbled into for lack of anything better to do. It wasn't strange that she had never married, though she had been close several times. No woman would behave like that, so why shouldn't she let them know what she was thinking?

'The fact is,' Bernard said, 'that I work hard, though

I don't make a song and dance about it. I get up at half past five, Saturday sometimes included, and set off for the office at six in the morning so as to avoid the rush hour. I often don't get home till nine in the evening, so poor Jenny doesn't see much of me, though there's little I can do about it, having my very good living to earn. I like my weekend, however, when I can get it. I don't travel the world as much as I used to, but being in an office means there is even more work. If I could find a secretary who would keep the same hours it would make things easier, but it's no use complaining about that these days.'

She took this as a dig at herself, though decided he hadn't intended it. 'No one seems all that high powered in the office of a small town solicitor.'

It was cool, but at least they were sheltered, refugees from the storm. A small motorboat was caught in the white tops of the waves. George, knowing where he would rather be, leaned back and lit a cheroot.

They chatted as if they were colleagues in the same big firm which, Gloria thought, in a way they might well be.

They were splayed on their beds after a shower, resting before dinner. 'Feel like a noggin?'

George pulled himself from a dream in which he was punching white crests, smashing each wave coming with malicious cat-like intention. 'Did I ever not?'

The click of the fridge, tinkle of glasses. Bernard stood tall and muscular in his liver-coloured pants. 'Say when.'

Bubble-bubble, toil and trouble. 'When. When, for God's sake. I don't want half a pint. Well, I do, but I won't be good for much if I swig that lot.'

He handed him the glass. 'You mean for Gloria?'

'It's you she's after, not me.'

'Truth to tell, I'm afraid she's after neither of us.'

'I expect you're right,' George said. 'Spinster type, or will be in a year or two. Cheers!'

'Cheers! Probably a lesbian.'

'That would be interesting.'

'You dirty old man.'

'She's a good sort, though.'

He sat down. 'Undoubtedly. The world's full of good sorts. Not good enough, though, to be a good sort. Good sorts are ten a penny. The world turns on them. Take Jenny, my dear wife. She's a good sort, but she's a lot of fun as well. It's those who are a lot of fun that I like – a dash of levity, humour and imagination. No chip on their shoulders. Spirit's what I'm talking about. How can you get through this goddamned life without a bit of fun? I don't mind work, but I like being alive, and I prefer a woman who also likes being alive. The same also applies to men, by which I mean my colleagues in the business – mostly men, unfortunately for me. But they also like being alive. We go out to dinner once a week, and knock back a dozen bottles between the six of us, a few Scotches beforehand, and the odd brandy afterwards. And always at a good club or restaurant. How we drive home afterwards I'll never know, though we've had no dead or wounded so far. But Gloria, I'm not sure she's ever been very keen on having fun. Maybe she is when she's back home, when one of the directors gets her on his knee, but here she seems too much taken up with the father she never knew, which can't promise much fun. I mean, here we are, two randy bastards ready to do our duty by her, and at this moment in time she's probably in her room sifting through old photographs and thinking about daddy. What bloody fun is that? Another?'

He was glad Bernard found her so dull. 'I didn't come out here to stay sober.'

'We never were before. At nineteen there were none so excessively pissed as us. Never came off patrol to drink less than a bottle of rum each, or put back a flagon or two of that South African poppy juice called van der Hum. Cheers!'

'Cheers! Still, don't be too hasty. One of us may get there yet.'

'I can't think so. But maybe I ought to give Jenny a tinkle before we go down.' Bernard reknotted his tie. 'I said I'd talk to her halfway through our stint.'

George stood. 'I'll wait downstairs, then.'

'Don't bother. It's only a courtesy call.' He dialled the dozen or so numbers. 'It's ringing. Must be near midday in Blighty. She'll be home for lunch. Hello? Darling? Raining here as well, till an hour ago, anyway. Who else? Of course it's me. Thought it was your boyfriend, eh? Ha-ha-ha! Of course I'm still sober. But what a miracle I'm able to jaw to you from all this way. What? You still love me? This is a wonderful line. As if you're in the next room. I wish you were. Yes, all going according to plan. George is fine. He's blotto, of course, but not in too bad shape, considering. He hasn't got Aids yet. Sends his love. Well, we're both trying, you know that. Yes, the food's fantastic. Can't go wrong. Dirt cheap, and tasty. No wine, but the whisky's a good year. Yes, we've got a big room between us. George snores, that's the only thing. He was motoring away all last night. Thought I was on the M25. I'm getting used to it, though. At least I'm not married to him. Only to you, thank God, and I'm missing you more than I can say. No, we haven't seen the old jungle yet, but we'll hire a car and get up there in a couple of days. Was it a snake skin or a tiger pelt you wanted? What? You love me? I love you too, darling. I'll show you how much when I get back. Can't wait. Funny being here, but wonderful all the same. It's the best idea you ever had. I'll love you forever. I always did. I know you do. Goodbye, sweetheart. I hope you're getting all my postcards. Many more are coming. Mmmmmmm! Bye, you lovely girl.'

The suppertime combo thrummed its melancholy tunes, and a woman of uncertain age and racial appearance, wearing a long black dress and heavily made up, sang in a full-throated wavering voice.

They ate shrimp and chicken salad, shared dishes of rice. The songs were not only forty years old, but went half a century back and even beyond. Gloria sipped her orange juice, looked now and again at the chanteuse, no more than glances, but each a concentrated appraisal of style or visage – or what? George wondered.

The singer wasn't old enough for her father to have listened to, or known, and she only felt sorry for her having to earn a few bob before an audience concerned in getting at their dinners. All the songs of the ages, or of the ages that mattered if you were still alive, came out as if the woman was inspired, and had been born knowing the tunes, as if the words were her own. 'Somewhere over the rainbow . . .' 'I'd like to get you on a slow boat to China.' 'A foggy day in London Town' and, most heartbreaking, 'Roses are blooming in Picardy'. In Muong, in this first class old colonial hotel, they played it night after night for the sentimental titillation of European visitors.

'And why not?' The three of them joined in clapping. 'They're wonderful old tunes,' Bernard said, 'all with good lyrics. Not like the eardrum-bursting pop rubbish with one inane line screamed out over and over again.'

George hadn't meant that at all, just that they were not of this world, not the real world, anyway.

'I'm happy enough to sit and listen,' Gloria said. 'But I wonder if young people would enjoy them?'

'Wouldn't know,' Bernard said. 'Nor much care.'

'If any were here they would probably be spellbound.' George felt that a school career had left him with some understanding of the kids today. 'As long as they weren't here with their parents, or elders. In which case they would feel obliged to dislike them. As they grew older, though, they'd probably be fascinated, like us.'

He was gratified when Gloria nodded agreement. She

saw how still they became at the band playing a Malayan tune. *Tara Bulang* it was called, or something like that, an old love song, George said, that was bashed out day after day from Radio Muong, as if megaphones had been fixed on the hilltops, coming from every wireless in camp and kampong. 'You old dog,' he laughed. 'You must have given her twenty dollars to sing it.'

'Fifty,' Bernard admitted. 'On our way in, but it was worth it. I've forgotten the words.'

'You roared them out word perfect when you were drunk, if I remember.'

' "I found a broken heart among my souvenirs," ' the woman sang, and with such a tune, and in the large dining room of a place like this, one would surely have seen the old rubber planter or tin miner, or prison governor, spending a few hours off from toil, or the eccentric sea captain gazing into space over the top of a whisky bottle while waiting for his ship to load. Timelessness was the essence of security and ease. Gloria broke into a lychee. 'I'm beginning to see why you loved the place when you were here before.'

Never was here, George was about to say, but Bernard took her up on it. 'After a gruelling patrol in the jungle we would call our bearer to get our smartest white drill ready. Then we would book out at the gate and commandeer a gharry to the ferry. Wonderful the breeze as we crossed the water. Junks with huge sails passing our track like old swans asleep. Must have read that somewhere. Sampans, too, cheery Malays giving us a wave as we leaned over the top rail, smoking our pipes, I expect. On the other side we took a trishaw to the Home and Colonial Hotel of course where the Armenian manager came out to greet us. "Ah, Mr George and Mr Bernard! It's so good to see you back, sirs. We have just had a special consignment of whisky from Fiji. Real Scotch. I've saved a few bottles especially for you." Just as well he never knew our surnames after we wrecked the place at the goodbye going-on-the-boat party. Otherwise we would have met your father under rather unpleasant circumstances, though at least we would have been able to tell you about him.'

The more they kept her amused the more she enjoyed being with them. It was strange that their prattle put an image of her father before her, or at least his photograph, which she took from her bag to show them: a hollow-cheeked sensitive face with balding swept-back hair, very short back and sides, eyes staring at horrors now fading away. He wore a tie and jacket, and very fine hands rested on his knees. George and Bernard weren't much older than he was when he died, and there was also the connection – real enough when they reminisced about their service, and even more when they exaggerated (which they clearly did, she supposed) – to when her father sat in a place like this. Not that either of them were like any father she could imagine, if only because of her father's job. 'It's a pity that same manager couldn't have been here to welcome you back.'

The band sugared out its rendering of 'Begin the Beguine'. George nodded. 'It's hard to know who the manager is these days, it's all so impersonal.'

'A very peculiar thing happened to me the first night here.' Bernard rested back on the two rear legs of his chair. 'We were having a few Scotches before dinner, feeling pretty mellow, to say the least. And when we were tucking in . . .'

George wondered what his old oppo would come up with now. 'About to.'

'Thank you for correcting me if I'm wrong.'

He lit one of his gnarled black sticks of tobacco. 'It's the least I can do.'

'You fussy old schoolteacher.'

'Anyway,' she said, 'get on with it.'

'We were sitting here prior to having a fair bash with the old chopsticks when – we were practically the only ones in that night – I saw a burly blackhaired Chinese kind of chap in a silk suit of the palest blue walking across the room, hand held out, and beaming a great Eddystone smile. He was coming straight for us, and I had a guttish feeling that I ought to run outside, leap over the wall, and swim for the mainland.'

'You left it a bit late.' George was at his most convincing. 'I'd have joined you in Bangkok, I suppose.'

'Too right I did. "Allow me to introduce myself," he said. "My name is Bernard Chong, and I have verifiable reason to believe that you are my father." I told him not to be so indisputably idiotic, and to leave us alone, or I would call the manager and have him ejected forthwith. His smile diminished not a wit, and when the cheeky devil sat at the spare chair he pulled out his wallet.'

She laughed. 'What now – you thought.'

'More than that. I knew what was coming. He was a rich man, to judge by the rings on his fingers, an expensive suit, and the sandalwood perfume, or whatever it was, with which he reeked. He took out a snapshot: "There, my dear father, sir, are you. And there, father, you one-time swine, is my mother." I looked – peered is the word – sweating, horrified, my hand shaking. It was indeed me, an inanely grinning youth, spruce and upright, curiously shy but callow to the nth degree, but at least my knees were brown, black shoes shining, creased trousers just out of the dhobi, shirt spotless. And there beside me – would you believe it? You'd better – was this Chinese girl smiling in her flowered trouser suit and holding a little parasol aloft as if she owned me. I remembered how I had abandoned her to get on the Blighty Boat. She was a nurse at the local hospital, a lovely person, and here was her offspring – my son, presumably – who I thought at any moment would bury an ivory-handled dagger into my chest for the wrong I had undoubtedly done his mother. I looked into his face. He had black hair, but otherwise there was some resemblance, though quite a fair way off under the fat which unmitigated prosperity had put on him. I could, in truth, barely hold back my tears.'

'Even I seemed almost moved,' George said.

' "What happened to her?" was all I wanted to know, feeling responsible at last. Bernard Chong took out his handkerchief. "She married, and had six more children. I was the guilty secret, and grew up with my grandparents in Taiping, who educated me, and put me into business selling motorbikes. I've sold more motorbikes than anyone in Malaysia, cheap low-powered Japanese machines that every young man wants. I also sell cars to those who get rich enough to discard their two-wheelers. But my mother is now a rich widow who lives in a fittingly luxurious bungalow in Kuala Lumpur. She'll be more than happy to know you are back. I'll telephone her soon. Perhaps you would like to see her?" '

'Quandary,' George said, 'was ever your middle name. All our dear Bernard is trying to do with such a story – and I'll guarantee its authenticity – is to suggest, in his subtle fashion, that your father may also have sundry mature offspring pulling rickshaws around the benighted streets.'

She stood, though George wondered why, and what else could she expect from a couple of silly bastards like them? Shouldn't react so stupidly to a joke. 'Sit down, and enjoy the fun.' When she did, he apologized. 'Sorry if I said anything unpleasant.'

She finished her orange juice. Must show I have some reason for staying, though she should have known that you always have to be on guard against those who can make fun of themselves so easily. 'I suppose I need to get used to your brand of humour.'

'It's taken me all my life,' Bernard said. 'And I'm still not sure whether I like it.'

George found her lack of humour interesting. 'Any white man out here could have children knocking about. Read Maugham, or Kipling or Conrad. A lot of funny business went on, you can bet. They all stayed at this hotel, though not at the same time.'

'A situation which don't bear thinking about,' Bernard said.

She wondered what specious yarn she could devise that would blast him to his backbone, though it was obvious that both were kippered and pickled beyond all proper feeling. She nevertheless felt relaxed at being with them, as if she had waited all her life to meet those who, by not seeming to care whether they offended her or not, made her question herself more than was usual. At the same time she felt more free and, while lulled by 'The bells are ringing for me and my gal', wondered which of the pair she would rather be with if they were stranded on an uncharted jungle island, or if they happened to be the last men on earth, looking on it as her good luck that she had no need to make up her mind.

Bernard's system of rectifying a mistake was to cover it by making things worse, a tactic, he found, which invariably succeeded. 'Why don't you come to our room for a double Scotch or so before bedtime?'

One minute they were funny buffers who hadn't a clue what effect their humour had on others, and the next you didn't know whether they weren't about to become a couple of rogue males whose volcanic intentions might turn scary. Bernard, tall and goodlooking, though plain and simple in his passions, which she knew well enough how to discourage, bothered her least; while George was bald and satyrish – no doubt a Taurus, like herself – who with his piercing grey eyes and pinpoint observations put her on the alert and reached parts of her she would rather not know about, or at least that he didn't get to know about. Holiday affairs were fine in their place, but not if they descended to a disturbing level and threatened to last more than was convenient. In any case, this wasn't a normal holiday – she had made that plain – and to get too mixed up with either of them, pleasant as they most of the time seemed, might not be wise.

And yet, wondering who she would choose if she did have to marry one was not a dull game to play between silences. The men she was attracted to rarely had more than one facet which was agreeable, and none satisfied all the conditions necessary for her wellbeing. Some tried to pretend that they had, guessing her needs more cannily, but it was never difficult to get rid of them because, with their veneer of sensibility, they lost heart soonest. Of these two, each possessed some qualities that might tempt her, though not for anything as stupid as marriage, because who would want to be caught up in something like that? The women she had known had all been married, funnily enough, and she had learned plenty to put her off. But these two chaps, with their so-called humour, undoubted experience, settled age, and ever-facile assumptions, might well have been an interesting proposition as one person, which thank God they were not, thus preventing her getting into anything foolish. She nevertheless surprised herself at saying to Bernard: 'All right, I'll come up for a few minutes. A small one, though. Then I must go to bed. I always have to read awhile before I can fall asleep.'

They took the wide staircase, not caring to encourage any Fundamentalist notions in the liftman. From the half-lit verandah George let them into the room, almost icily cool after the sauna heat outside, and the exertion of the ascent.

Bernard played host, excellent at that, George smiled from his slouch in the armchair, knowing it was wise to give jobs to those who did them best. 'You've poured me too much.' Gloria put half into his glass. 'I didn't agree to a deluge.'

'Sorry about that.' He sat on the edge of the bed, his first gulp rectifying the matter. 'Funny thing being in this room with you, Gloria. Even more peculiar, I suppose, being here with old George. The last time I was here it was with a young George, in the days when we arsed around like nobody's business. Luckily, when we had guns in our hands we had a corporal close by to see we didn't go mayhem. And look at George now. Kind and right thinking, considerate, full of fine feeling. Same with me, give or take a knock, or a harsh word. But what I would like to know is: what made us into the lambs of society, when we'd been such unthinking killers?'

'A change of clothes?' George suggested. 'The colour of your braces has a lot to answer for. A homely parlour instead of a billet, maybe. Even a hotel room, stamped out on the same universal template, has a knack of keeping one civilized. Funny indeed to be back in Malaya, though now that the curtains are closed we could be in a hotel anywhere in the world.'

He was surprised to see Gloria sip, and then swallow the whole of her drink. 'I know I'm in the tropics,' he went on, 'with that aircon, as the natives call it, rattling away. All rooms are the same, when you think about it. They have chairs, a table, beds, wardrobes. Can't be different, can they? It's the outside that matters, and that's never like anywhere else in the world. And all hearts have the same bruises, scars, basic reactions, in my experience.'

Bernard raised his eyebrows at such philosophizing. Her views came close to George's, but because she distrusted hers she saw no reason not to distrust his. Yet at least they provided the logic for getting to know people, and because he expressed such views with confidence she thought him a wiser person, till she realized it was only because he was older.

Bernard threw the cork across the room. 'There's just enough of this spa juice left for another or two. Big ones, of course.'

Gloria pushed her glass forward. 'Cheers!'

'You can say that again.' He was gratified at getting her into the game. 'Cheers! – you lovely girl!'

George's eyes lost focus, a sure sign that he was going into the land of one-too-many.

'I'm beginning to wonder why I'm here,' she said.

Bernard gargled his fire water. 'We invited you for a nightcap, remember? I don't know what George intended. He's a very unpredictable dark horse.'

'I mean, in Malaya. I think I came for a rather shallow reason.'

'Maybe we should all leave well alone,' George thought. She stretched out her legs, and his polaroid snapshot observed how very shapely they were.

'I for one,' said Bernard, 'am having a good time.'

'So am I,' she slurred her words, 'the more I forget why I came.'

'We should all renounce such reasons.'

Bernard laughed. 'I second that emotion. Then we could have a whale of a time. Malaya today, and Bangkok in the middle of next week tomorrow.' He hoisted the bottle, and dealt out the remainder, a tall slug for each.

'You only learn from having a good time,' George said. 'Never from a bad experience. Cheers!'

She played naïve. 'Do you think so?'

'People like us, I mean. A good time is hard to come by, but when it does it loosens one up no end. *In vino veritas* we learn painlessly about ourselves and others.'

'Hedonism forever!' Bernard, from looking at his face in the glasstopped table, felt ballbearings under his feet and had to sit down.

'My mother always lectured me,' she said, 'about how good my father had been. But the other day, after lounging on the beach, I hired a taxi and went to look at the prison, where he was the governor.' She slumped, but before George could get across, straightened herself, a forceful effort to escape the fog after stupidly drinking so much of their poison. 'Maybe you're right, and a good time is the only priority.' She regretted her inane speech, which made things worse than if she had said nothing.

'Someone had to do the job.' George put his glass aside. 'Such places aren't always full of innocent idealistic people. Maybe some of them are, but all the same . . .'

'Oh for God's sake stop bumbling. You're getting pissed.' Bernard reached for his tumbler, finished the drink, fell onto the bed, and began to snore. Gloria gave strict orders to her arm not to put any more whisky to her lips, but it mutinied, and she took two genteel swigs.

'My father was a Methodist preacher,' George said. 'A good man, and I never realized how much I respected him till he was dead. Even worse, I never knew how much he loved me, and how little I was capable of returning it. Too late, of course. Everything is always too late – even at the time, when you realize that one day it will be.'

Bernard sat up, took off his tie, and one shoe. 'Sorry I spoke so harshly, old man. You're my best friend, and I love you. I put that on record.' Then he fell back into an even louder snore.

'The prison was such a grim building,' she said. 'Maybe terrible things happened there. And they still are. But did I come eight thousand miles to hate myself? I'm thirty-six, so you'd think I'd have more sense.'

George held her hand. 'I don't remember any age being especially noted for common sense, and I'm sure there isn't such an age to look forward to.' He laughed. 'Certainly not in my case.'

Bernard was settled, as if forever, on his stomach. 'Hear-hear! I second that . . .'

'I think I'd better see you to your room.'

'I can manage,' she said.

He wasn't at all sure that she could, nor indeed that he was capable of fatherly assistance, though she had only to walk along the verandah, broach a flight of stairs, and navigate the same distance along the second floor. 'I'm off for a stroll by the sea wall,' he said. 'I like to commune with myself a bit before bedtime.'

In the corridor she said: 'I'll go with you, if I may.'

'What about your book?'

She smiled under the dim light. 'I think the print will be too small tonight.'

'He did rather ply us.'

'He plied himself more. He seems very unhappy.'

The idea silenced him. If she was right, and he thought she might well be, then why hadn't he noticed? Bernard who always seemed happy was suddenly unhappy, and himself, whom he considered hardly ever to have been happy, was certainly not classified by her as among the despondent. 'Bernard and I only communicate on one level.'

'So I gather.'

'It suits us, but you'd find him a different person on his own.'

'Oh, I certainly don't think he's a fool. Far from it.'

He leaned against the parapet, patches of water lit by the moon. 'I suppose everyone enjoys knowing one person in the world with whom they don't have to be on guard all the time. Bernard and I don't compete at the same business, long for the same woman, covet each other's possessions, or are even keenly ambitious in our different careers. We once shared a couple of years' active service, which stamped a sameness onto us that forty years hasn't blotted out. What the reason is, when most men have forgotten, or would remember it only with embarrassment, I can't think. It may be superficial, or even downright puzzling, but the relationship goes on because of an ease we can't find anywhere else.'

A breeze corrugated the water, hissed in the palm fronds, a splash out at sea, but no one there. He enjoyed talking now that he had found someone to listen, unless she was being tolerant only because her senses were muffled by whisky. No matter, though he suddenly felt too tired to continue standing. An illuminated container ship slid down channel, comforting in that they were not alone. 'It's a privilege to be able to work all one's life, but it's those conflicts which are unnecessary that cause the anguish, though maybe without such anguish it would be impossible to work at all, the anguish being the oil in the machine.' Hard to stop making redundant remarks to someone he wanted least in the world to think him a fool. 'I got through my life by seeing every failure, each onset of anguish, as a test of character that I had to pass. That helped.'

She found it uncanny how close his thoughts were to hers, and how comforting that the similarity did not alarm her. Instead of one ship she saw two, one for each eye. Two moons and a double horizon crossed her line of vision like a dead straight road. But there was no road. 'I think I must lie down.'

'I'll see you to your door.'

She moved away, afraid of vomiting. 'Looks better if I go on my own.' He was far away, a world gone, and a world gained when he came sharply back. Good job someone was there, now that she had made such a fool of herself. 'But thank you, and Bernard, for a lovely evening.'

Would she get there, or would she not? Her sway was subtle, but he was damned if he would track her to make sure, though in five minutes he might reconnoitre, to confirm that she hadn't curled up in some corner.

She didn't know herself whether she would get there, except that it was worth the test, stiffening her legs so that she'd be taken for lame by a sympathetic onlooker, and not for blind drunk by anyone else. Hand closing on the balustrade, the steps counted themselves, but she caught the nearest rail to avoid sideslip. At the first floor she paused, gripped her endless sway to begin the second phase. As long as she moved she wouldn't fall, but why hadn't she told that to herself before?

seven

The battery of four guns defended them from the seaward side, but the black-mouthed bombard would spit its evil load vertically, so that it would come down and obliterate defenders and attackers alike. 'They used to guard the place against pirates marauding up and down the coast,' Bernard said. 'They still operate between the islands. Tankers and container ships are so big that pirates slip on board and get to the bridge with their Kalashnikovs before the officers know what's what. They make off with the valuables in the safe, plus whisky, hi-fis and cigarettes. Shipping companies advise the officers and crew to give in gracefully. They can't take the actual cargo, after all. It's too big. If they robbed local ships the government would wipe them out rightaway. Only big fatcat Western ships. Just like they pirate our books. We lose millions a year. We used to sell books to 'em, but now they get hold of a pricey title and print it by the thousand in their backyards. Don't pay us a penny. Not much we can do about it. The governments don't care, either, because it saves on foreign exchange. If I had my way we'd send a gunboat and hang a few of the villains outside every highrise. But we can't do it these days, more's the pity. We saved 'em from communism, but you can't expect them to behave according to the rules. Not our rules, anyway.' He mopped up the rest of his breakfast. 'I wonder what's happened to Gloria, after our mini-binge of last night?'

'Don't look at me like that.'

'You dirty old man.'

'She's probably eating in her room.'

'When I got undressed you were AWOL.'

'I was just having a quiet smoke downstairs.'

'What was she like?'

'We chatted for ten minutes, then she went up. I hope she got there. If I'd been a gentleman I would have seen her to her door, but she positively discouraged me.' He lit his after-breakfast cheroot while Bernard read the newspaper. Memories of the old days made it impossible to forget why he was here, but the black and white film of then and the Technicolor production of now were slowly merging. Maybe by the time they left the difference would be minimal. 'What do you say: that we cancel our three days in Kuala Lumpur, and stay the rest of our time up here?'

'Listen to this lovely yarn from Manila. I suppose it's true, though you can't always believe what's printed, as well I know. "A couple could not be separated after the sexual act, and had to be taken to the hospital, where they were sedated. Then they were able to part. The penis of the woman's lover had become so swollen that he couldn't get out. People were queueing at the hospital to see them." I wonder what the woman's husband said when he heard the news? It actually says that she was married.'

'That would be a rather tall story,' George said, 'if it didn't sound like the marriage of East and West.'

'Read it for yourself. It's too good a tale for me to make up, though maybe some journalist did.' The paper folded, reading glasses back in their case. 'Scrub KL, did you say? A suggestion like that calls for another pot of coffee.'

George flicked a hand for the waiter. 'I'll have one, as well.' A crow stepped onto a recently vacated table, and flew off with a Danish pastry.

'They're getting bolder,' Bernard said. 'I'd better watch my camera. The local lads train them like the gannets for fishing, I shouldn't wonder.'

'It'll be a bit of a bore, walking our feet off between skyscrapers and government offices in Kuala Lumpur,' George said, 'when we could go on enjoying ourselves in this comparatively cushy billet. In any case we haven't been to the mainland yet to take a look-see at the primeval forest. If we hang on here for the extra few days we can hire a car and drive to the spot where we set off after those bandits. I wouldn't mind dipping my toes into the virgin jungle again. Jenny said we could change the arrangements according to how we found things. If we keep our room here, we phone the hotel at KL to cancel, then book our plane direct to Singapore. The lovely ladies behind the desk will do the necessary paperwork.'

George was surprised at his skill in laying out such persuasions, and justifications. Let's call them reasons – coming almost without thought, almost inspired, you might say, as if even he should have suspected their glibness instead of feeling pleased.

'Better give me a moment to think about it,' Bernard said as they drank their coffee. 'So you want to see more of Gloria?'

Hope waned because there seemed so little possibility. He had spent all his life keeping hope under control. You could taunt it perhaps, damp it down certainly, throw it away on occasion, because only if a spark of hope turned into a fire could it be said to have been valid. You only realized it was hope in looking back, by which time it might have brought too much trouble in its wake for him to believe it had begun as a pleasant sensation. 'Not necessarily.'

Bernard knew better. 'She's very personable, and getting more so all the time. You have a good effect on her, I must say.'

'Life's too short to stake anything on that.'

'Think more of the bloody particular, old boy. Not so much of Life-this and Life-that. Much better for you. And for me, as far as that goes.'

'I know, but I'm still being nagged by this search for the old days. Might as well be at Benidorm, or some such place, because here I sit, looking across at palm trees on the mainland, and it's a wonderful sight, but it's really like something I'm seeing on TV. I remember what it was like before, and try to see it as I think it ought to be, but it doesn't come back into my heart.'

Bernard tapped a tune on his cup. 'Same here, more or less, but there's nothing to be done about it.'

No sense worrying – a fool's game, if you played it knowing that you need not do so. But desire knotted his stomach, and George had no choice, fight as he might, scoff as he knew he should, except to cohabit with the inexplicable wish to recover something beyond lifeless photography. He suggested that having met Gloria only confused their attempts to get at the past.

'Five people were killed in a fire at Ipoh, it says here. A whole family gone.' Bernard shuffled the newspaper. 'She might be thinking the same. But me, I'm just a lifelong syba-rite. If the past comes back, all well and good. If it doesn't, it's a nice holiday. Let's do a spot of shopping.' He stood up. 'Then I'll buy something else for my lady-wife.'

A police notice said that you could be fined five hundred dollars for dropping litter, and on the mile-long stretch of sand by the Beach Tree Hotel they saw only one discarded can. 'The local anarchist spends a bomb every morning before breakfast,' Bernard remarked, 'yet doesn't have a cent in his pocket.' The place was so empty it was hard to know where to sit. 'Still, it wouldn't be a bad idea to try such a scheme back home. The amount of rubbish people throw around is disgusting.'

George's heart burned after a modest lunch. 'A law like

that would put even law-abiding people's backs up.' He paused, and a satisfactory belch eased his progress along the sand. 'If you enacted such laws they'd stop inventing things. Malaya might have clean beaches, but I'd like to know what they've invented.'

'Don't strictly see the connection, old boy.'

Neither did he, but felt a need to wander from the beaten track of automatic agreement. They sat under the partial shade of a pine, watching a shoal of black and yellow sailing boards manoeuvring on the water. George read the tourist guidebook, wondering what there was still to see on the island. 'It says that people from Cuba, China, Israel and Albania can't get visas to come here.'

Bernard used the field glasses to bring the surfers close, hoping to see a tall blonde topless dolly parting the waves like Aphrodite being reborn into the twentieth century. 'They'll have to stop that if they want to ginger up the tourist business. Come one and come all, it ought to be.'

'Another item says that the *gunong* we shinned up after the bandits was a legendary mountain. A king lived on its slopes, who had fangs and drank human blood.'

'All I can say to that is it's a good job we didn't know at the time. "Don't want to go up there, sergeant." "Why not, lad?" "Wouldn't like to say, sergeant." "You must have a reason, soldier." "It's dark up there." "Come on, man, what's biting you?" "Well, sarge, there's a dragon up there, with fangs. It eats men like us for breakfast. We haven't even got our knees brown." "Come on, you lily-livered bastards," the sergeant bawls, crashing into the undergrowth. And up we went. Frightens me when I think about it. I hope we don't bump into the Old Devil when we go over to the mainland and do another recce.'

There was, as ever, cumulus over Gunong Rimau, clouds that never seemed to move, though a wind blew against the forested cape of Muka Head. Two sampans motoring by left neat coils of foam. George wanted to walk endlessly through the forest, or swim till he lost strength and went under. But he lay mindlessly on the sand, eyes half closed, without the will to stand up.

'Bliss it was that day to have no worries,' Bernard said, and was asleep as soon as he lay down. A jumble of cloud canopied the sea which seemed empty of ships until Burma. But fair weather could change in a moment. George walked half a mile up the beach, passing two white girls all but naked on the sand. Coming back he spotted Gloria, at a table of the hotel.

She thought he was going to walk by, whether or not he'd seen, but he veered towards her. All morning she had looked around the hotel, feeling stupid because so bereft at his absence. 'When I couldn't find you I supposed you'd left already for Kuala Lumpur.'

The stay had been cancelled, their room kept on at the Home and Colonial. No problem, the girl clerk said. Just how they liked it: to have your own way yet not be a bother, smiles all round at the inconvenience, even when they got onto the phone. 'What a pity it's not like this back home,' Bernard had said. 'Maybe it is if you're a foreign tourist, though I doubt it. It takes intelligence to be efficient and polite. The high standard out here is positively depressing.'

George wondered whether she meant only him. 'We decided to finish our time here, in paradise.' He knew it was up to her to ask him to sit, but he did so without invitation. An intermittent hissing of wind in the trees, and the softer smiting of breakers, both sounds playing with each other. The cool whistle of birds, and an occasional human voice sounded against their talk.

'I'd like something to happen,' she said, 'but how does one go about it? When I'm at home leading a so-called normal life it doesn't bother me. Funny, that it should only get at me when I come out here.'

She had a glass of orange juice, so he ordered a bottle. 'Best leave it alone, then,' he said. 'You can only go at the pace of your own temperament, and act within its limits.'

'You're right, I expect.' She was disappointed, at not hearing something else.

'Safer that way, at least.'

'I don't know about that,' she laughed. 'And if I'm right it gives me no pleasure.' We're similar, she thought. So similar that she was wary, disturbed by her openness to him.

Another motorized sampan split the peace. He was unwilling to think before he spoke, as he had done all his life. 'We're thinking of going to the place from where we set off on a patrol into the jungle forty years ago.' Just to stand there and look at it, not hoping for a revelation, or a memory to come back that'll knock us off our feet, but to see what it was that we went into as twenty-year-olds. 'Do you want to come?'

He wished he hadn't made the offer. They weren't finally settled on it, in any case, and Bernard might not want to include her. He hoped she would laugh at such an outlandish idea, but she said: 'Do you mean it?'

'I offered, didn't I?'

Her smile of pleasure, the first he had seen, told him that he had lost. 'I'll come, then,' she said, 'if you really don't mind.'

'For my part, I'd be delighted.'

'Thought I'd find you two,' Bernard said, brushing sand off his chest. 'Why don't you come for a swim instead of playing jaw-jaw?'

'I've talked Gloria into coming with us when we go to take a look at the old jungle,' George said. 'You don't mind, I hope?'

He sat down. 'Terrific. Must have a drink, or I'll shrivel even more. We'll hire a car, and get packed lunches.'

Wanting to be certain, she asked when.

'On Monday,' Bernard said. 'We'll go over by the bridge.'

The taxi man played bongo music on his radio so loud on

136

the way into town that no conversation was possible. Luckily he was an expert driver, and threaded the motorbikes without killing anybody, getting them to the hotel in time for tea.

The dining room was cooler than the outside terrace, but the gloom settled over them. Bernard asked for cake with the pot of tea, and the waiter came back after ten minutes to say there wasn't any. 'What? No bloody cake in a hotel like this? What would Somerset Maugham and Noel Coward have said? As for Captain Conrad, by God he would have blasted you.'

'I'm sorry, sir. Just no cake today.'

Bernard's face was more choleric than usual, lips down-curving. Something had upset him but no one knew what. 'Send a boy out to buy some.'

The waiter stayed, as if he hadn't cushioned his guest's annoyance to the full. 'No one to go, sir.'

'There should be a waiter for every guest in the hotel, like in the old days.'

'Every five it was, sir. People don't want to be waiters any more. Or they not fit to be waiters.' He smiled, then walked away.

'Bloody pity,' Bernard called after him.

'Oh shut up,' Gloria said. 'It's not his fault.'

'I should have called the manager.' He wouldn't let go. 'Given the bugger a dressing down. Your father would have clapped him in jail for a couple of weeks.'

'No he wouldn't. There was a law against that kind of thing. He would have said nothing, and drunk his tea.'

'Like us,' George said, pouring. 'But where's the milk? I see no milk.'

'We'll have it black.' She shrugged. 'Better without, any-way.'

Bernard wondered how the hell they'd got into this, and George knew it for a sign that they were coming back to life, out of the brotherhood and into the world. Who could say what kind of a world it would be, should the worst occur and they get accustomed to it? Hard to imagine he would live to see the day. But if he didn't, he would litigate with God and grind him into the dust. Either that, or he would, as his father used to say, Job himself with resignation, and gain eternal favour.

The broken pavement zigzagged up and down, between tree roots which forced them out to face oncoming traffic along the straight treelined road. But they stayed side by side, and whenever possible she held his arm. 'I don't know why,' he said, 'but I like being with you.'

He was either too simple, or too honest – probably both. 'You're very flattering.'

Well, he hadn't expected her to be pleasant about his thoughtless remark. 'I've decided to speak plainly for the rest of my life!'

She regretted that she had used the wrong tone for the way she felt. 'How else would I want it?' Her voice at least was friendly, belying the words.

They were on the island jogging route: a couple of Chinese, an Indian, and a European elbowed by, claiming priority due to their exertions. 'On the other hand I'm happy being with you and not talking,' he said.

'Don't, then, though I suppose that also might be flattery.' She couldn't stop, but earnestly wanted to. 'Is that the only way you know how to talk to a woman?'

'You're giving me a hard time.'

'Or talk to anyone, come to that. But what makes you think I don't like flattery?'

'I don't. For myself I wouldn't mind it at all, so why should you? That's the only way I have of gauging a remark, to apply it to myself. My so-called intuition, if I ever had any, must have been scorched out long ago, so all I can do is play around with permutations and hope I gauge mine and other people's feelings right. Emotional snakes-and-ladders, if you like.'

'You don't do too badly with it.'

'Thank you.' He walked between her and the road, keeping his haversack on the inside should one of the motorcyclists veer in to snatch it, as he'd heard they did in Italy. But all the riders seemed intent on getting to where they were going. A young man smiled under his visor because he had a girl behind. George told her his thoughts.

'You're very distrustful.'

'I feel that makes two of us.'

'Could be.'

'I'm protective towards you, though it's got nothing to do with our different ages.' He sensed the lift of her eyebrows. 'Men and women have to protect each other, because who else will? My wife and I fought and competed every minute of our lives. In our dreams as well, I shouldn't wonder. I always knew something was wrong, and so did she, but we could never do anything about it. Consequently it was hell the whole time, our lives passing before we could do the sensible thing and separate.'

'What a horrible waste.'

He was saturated with sweat. At the traffic island the road turned towards the beach. 'Since I expect to live forever I can't think it was bad for me. Many people live that way, catting and dogging it, to use a phrase of my father's, yet guarding each other from the outside world. Hell is a very protective environment.'

He talked as he thought – how else could you? – cunning in that he felt it might endear him to her, but also unsure of himself as she also obviously was, because he didn't give a damn, as if being shut off from the past showed more clearly what he wanted.

Crowds converged onto the beach for the Great Dragon Boat Race. The road was lined with food stalls, tempting smells at eleven in the morning whether you'd had a hotel breakfast or not. There was nothing to flaw the blue sky and the straight palm coast of the mainland, and the wall of inland mountains holding down the heat. 'I suppose your jungle must be somewhere over there.'

'Precisely fixed. I have my old maps to tell us. The mountains look smooth from here, but they're covered with huge trees two hundred feet high, so close that their canopies cut out all light and it's almost dark underneath, even at midday. I remember it well. We came down from the jungle exactly forty years ago – out of the House of Bondage, you might suppose.'

People sat on stands between the concrete parapet and the water to watch the boats go through their paces. A pop band under the trees beat an indiscriminate spectrum of sound into everyone's eardrums. Longboats with fearsome dragon prows pulled up onto the sand looked comical till they were hauled a hundred yards out and, a dozen half-naked men flashing their paddles, cut along the glassy water like knives through linoleum.

Three boats ran the quarter-mile course under full colours. 'Never seen this before,' George said when the cheers and megaphonic comment diminished.

She put an arm over his shoulder. 'It was worth coming for. I don't suppose we'll know how much till we get back home.'

Bernard stood on the sand and aimed his camera at another dash of the boats. Teams had come from all over Malaysia, even from New Zealand. 'Want a fiver on the Kiwis?'

'Technicolor memories,' George said. 'This time they'll certainly see us out.' War canoes charged into action with whooping and cheering, dragonheads up front.

'Wouldn't like them coming at me with their swords and axes.' Bernard's camera was silent behind the noise. 'That's why they're so go-ahead out here. Education and intelligence, plus hard work. They've struck an equilibrium between the ultra-modern and the barbaric.' He took out the finished reel and reloaded. 'Got the edge on us all right.'

People were cheerful on fiesta day, though George wondered at so many police and army wagons. Were they there for drugs, gamblers and immoral practices, or to control larger crowds expected in the afternoon?

The winners of each heat beat their paddles into a rhythm of triumph, boats levelling towards a line of flags. Gloria stood apart, her own small camera lifted, hair showing from her armpits. She wore a halter, and shorts and sandals, nothing outstanding about her face and figure perhaps, but George wanted to see her naked, lie with her, never let go, though her independence and remoteness promised little chance. Since his marriage he had found it hard to get used to living from hour to hour. But the eternal state of chagrin and emptiness had been honed up as a way of existence, not unpleasant, though he wondered whether he would ever be able to unlock himself from it. He drew back from such futile yearning to be with her, yet pleased that he could still fall in love. Hoping she wouldn't resent the intrusion on the obvious race of her private thoughts he said: 'Would you like to drink something?'

'Love to, if we can share another coconut.' The woman lopped the top off with a hatchet and gave them two straws. 'I didn't know I was so thirsty.' She wiped the dew from her temples, and almost lost her grip on the straw when smiling for him alone. Reaching his free hand, she stroked it for a moment, then held the fleshy bulb of the coconut to go on drinking – with this chap she liked perhaps more than she should, a long time since she had felt so free and loving with a man.

By the cookstalls their chair legs sank a few inches into the sand. A plate of noodles, prawns and beanshoots came up for a dollar each. George, with an unusual hunger, took soup with vermicelli, prawns and bits of pork.

'Going it a bit, aren't you?' Bernard said.

'They don't call it Guzzlers Row for nothing.' He fetched a cup of chrysanthemum tea for Gloria, an infusion of a neutral shade, but the refreshing taste pleased her. Sitting back to smoke, he only realized how exhausted his spirit had been now that he was coming back to life. Worn by the long fight, he was getting into the self he had always known to be there.

Bernard looked around. 'What a combination of sea and sport! And all these pleasant people, not to mention the superb grub. Clever Jenny for arranging it all!' He sniffed. 'Are those black sock-juice cigars still all right, old boy? He used to send everybody running for the sickbay forty years ago. Cleared the Orderly Room in no time.'

On the water, longboats formed a line, a hiatus of peace which, though it couldn't last, showed that living need not be such pain. 'Never felt better.'

'Nor me,' Gloria said. 'Isn't it strange?'

Such moments were more welcome because they could not last, memorable for their brevity. Her body was close in the taxi going back, their hands together and resting on his knee. He wore long trousers, and wanted to put their hands on her knees, which were bare, but he sensed that such a move might be presuming too much, yet also that it was hardly necessary any more.

At the reception counter she called out the number when asking for her key. 'I'm going up to rest awhile.'

George heard the figures, but was not finally sure that she had meant him to. The young woman who handed their room key to Bernard, without them having to state the number, must also have been familiar with Gloria's, but Gloria had asked for it that way.

'And there's a letter for you, Mr Missenden,' the receptionist said. 'It was forwarded from the hotel you would have gone to in Kuala Lumpur.'

Bernard gave his charming smile, which George had to admit most women must find attractive. 'We only told them a couple of days ago. Who would believe in such wonderful efficiency?'

She handed it to him. 'We like to do our best for our guests.'

'It's beyond the call of duty. You're truly terrific.'

'You go up.' George would let him read the passionate letter from Jenny in solitude. 'I'll get myself some tea outside.' He expected him to say 'Oh come on, didn't we used to read our mail in the billet no matter how many blokes were around?' But he said: 'If that's how you feel. Her room was three-two-three, wasn't it? At least my memory says so.'

'Go to hell.' George laughed. 'There's nothing further from my mind.' Not exactly true, though why it wasn't he wouldn't take the trouble to imagine. He knew the number as well as Bernard.

The tea was lousy today, but he would never tire of looking at the flat treelined coast where he had passed two years of his life. The longer he gazed the more irritated he became with those half-perceived memories playing so hard to get and, at last, meaning less and less. The crows were quiet, the clever ones no doubt gone elsewhere for richer loot. Four Aussie airmen at a table by the pool, all bottles empty, did not know what else to say to each other, looked in the same direction as himself and seemed equally bored. He was empty of thought, the closest he could get at the moment to a kind of peace. Flagging for his bill, he saw Gloria come out of the lobby, and felt an excitement which denied his relaxation, though he loved her for taking it away.

She had changed into shirt and skirt. 'So this is where you are?'

'Easy to find me.'

She sat down, turned the cup around in its saucer till the handle faced her. 'I was waiting for you upstairs.'

'Is it too late?'

The smile was forced, something uncertain about it. 'Give me time to get back.'

The Aussies observed him going into the hotel. It's happened, he thought, pausing on the shabbily carpeted stairs, just like that.

He rang the bell, and heard her get up to let him in. The room was smaller than the one he shared with Bernard, a double bed but no view over the sea, a crop of postcards scattered on the desk. Before he could take in anything else, and the moment the door swung shut, she held him, and he kissed her lips. 'You kept me waiting,' she smiled.

Was he the first one who ever did? A mere accident, a hiccup in time, he was ever unsynchronized – he said.

'So was I.' Her head and heart were always separate till the vital moment. Now they were one, and she knew he was ready, that he wouldn't mind that she had broached the issue, him being older and with enough understanding to push surprise or embarrassment aside. Would he say he loved her? Too experienced for that, she didn't wonder. Nothing mattered as she pulled the bedclothes back, and parted herself from him to go through a formal undressing, a ritual in which he joined so that they could lie down together with a passion that at the moment anyway seemed new to them both.

'Open up, old man.'

He had rung three times, silence and strange noises the only response.

'Go away.'

'Stop arsing around' – as if a bit of the old lingo might do the trick, unless he was so chagrined at his having been with Gloria that he would never forgive him, and make him pay to the limit for what he considered his unparalleled luck. But Bernard was too good a sport for that kind of thing, if George had ever been able to read anyone's character at all. He gave another press at the bell button. 'Come on, there's still time for a few noggins before dinner.'

From a dead voice to the relatively normal: 'Hang on a second.'

'Who's in there, you old ram?' The girl from behind the desk, he wouldn't be surprised. As for himself, he was not the same person who had left the room that morning, an unfamiliar sense of transformation. He should have known something decisive was about to occur, but because he hadn't he had made it even more likely to happen. Fate only took you properly by the throat when you were in too vague a mood to realize what was going on, stuck in your own mire. All his life his thought processes had even been parallel to his own track, which was perhaps why his wife had always maintained that he could worry though not think. He was only capable of recognizing something after it had happened. 'I'm sweating to death out here. I need a bit of the old aircon on my skin, not to mention a shower and a shot of whisky.'

No sound of feet coming towards it, the door swung inwards. Bernard backed away, a hand over his face, the weight of some as yet unexplained disaster settled on rounded shoulders. He had lost his straightened back, but what, George wondered, had got at him? Stomach cramps that made him suspect cancer? A stab of indigestion like a scalpel at the heart? Couldn't be. Bernard was no hypochondriac.

'Knackered, I'm afraid.' His granulated tone was unrecognizable. 'Only temporary, though.' He nodded towards the bottle, and half glass of whisky on the table. 'Oiling the biggest jolt to my system I've ever had.' He moved back towards the bed, afraid of falling.

'What's amiss?'

'The old engine's coked up.' He let his hand drop, revealing lips bitterly down, eyes out of focus, hair meshed. 'I seem to have received a "Dear John" letter. Jenny's lit off.'

'Impossible.' He felt a fool, nothing better to say. 'I don't believe it. Stop pulling my leg.'

'Scooted, at fifty, and I had no idea it was in the offing.

Pissed off with a solicitor's clerk twenty years younger, who's left his wife and two kids.'

Little pages of black and blue bunting – flags without strings – were strewn between bed and bathroom, closely written on both sides. She had really let him have it. 'What an awful thing.'

Knowing where they all were, Bernard swooped on page one, and stood up to read. 'Just listen to this: "Dear Bernard, I've written this letter so many times – in my mind, but also now and again on paper, over the years – that I know how to end it but hardly where to begin. And now that I have started I don't know how to go on, though when I've finished the broad picture you'll be able to fill in the details without me having to tell you. At least you're out of the country, and won't be coming in to look over my shoulder. By the time you are back in England I'll be far enough away for you not to know where I am, because, because, because . . ." '

George lost count at the twentieth 'because', then stepped in. 'All right, old man?'

A smile, as if after being three weeks on a raft in the middle of the ocean sort of smile, came with much effort. He sat on the bed, bereft. 'Both of us had a little bit on the side over the years, and why not? I've generally known. I suppose she did as well, but we kept going. I'd never have gone off with one of my girlfriends.'

She had broken the rules, and no mistake. 'It often hits a woman harder than a man.' George poured a chota peg, knowing he sounded at his most banal, possibly irrelevant. But he would say whatever came to mind because Bernard wanted talk of any sort, more than nodding commiseration as from a rubber dog in the back window of a car. 'They take things more seriously.'

'At nearly fifty?'

George was embarrassed because he thought Bernard might start crying – again, he assumed. 'Nobody's past it, ever, even at eighty.' And she was an attractive woman, fifty or not.

'Takes some believing, but that bloody letter convinces me.' He nodded, all cares momentarily gone. 'At least the children are grown up. Won't they be amused? I suppose she's sent them separate letters, though none as long as mine. Amended them on the word processor, my little present for her last birthday. At least she wrote mine by hand. I always told her I took no notice of personal letters bashed out on the typewriter.' Shoulders like a loaded sack, hands back at his face.

'Will you be getting an earlier plane home?'

There were tear scars on his cheeks. 'Wouldn't miss our bit of jungle bashing for the world. In any case, there's no point getting back to the scene of the crime too soon. I might be tempted to go for the shot gun.'

George imagined him, wearing battle fatigues and survival gear, tracking through fields and woods to reach their secret cottage, face blackened, pouches bulging, both barrels at the business angle. No man was an island, you could say that again, and he did – or an angel for that matter. He lit a cheroot, breaking the no smoking rule agreed on for the room. 'There's a law against the old one-two with powder and shot. We'd both be dead by now if there wasn't. I know overpopulation is a curse, but I don't think that's quite the way to cure it. It would only get rid of the go-ahead people, and the world can't afford that, especially the Western world.'

He felt remarkably relaxed before Bernard's misfortune, which was just as well, because joining in the misery would only make it worse. It seemed to be working, till Bernard said angrily: 'Can you imagine, planning her little *coup* for the last two years? I thought she had been devious out of love, springing this trip on me, but within that plan had been another little plan, a time bomb set to go off when I would least be able to do anything to gum up the works. And I thought I knew her! That's what makes it so hard to take. She packs up and goes just when I realize that I don't know her at all, and not giving me any more time to get to know her! God, what a bitch! I'll never forgive her!'

'She's got you forever if you don't.'

'I suppose I never came to grips with the habits of the modern world, damn me.'

'Could have happened a hundred years ago. There's no modern or old-fashioned where something like this is concerned.'

'Positively Machiavellian.'

'That's about it.'

During the silence Bernard considered the situation, and took another long dose of drink. 'Won't have to hide my affairs any more, and that's a fact. But don't tell me every cloud has a silver lining, either.'

'What if she comes back to you? It often happens.'

'No hope or fear of that. You haven't read the whole letter. Still, you've been through this yourself. You're a little bit in advance of me. You always were, if I remember.'

'Mine wasn't so neat. Years of wrench, all ends hanging loose and bloody. Neither of us went to somebody else, which shows how bad it was. I'm probably not recovered yet, though I think it'll be easier from now on.' Which was the closest he could get to telling him, though Bernard was too much in the lair of the wounded to take it in.

But he wasn't. There were no flies on him, though there were numerous marks where the buggers had nipped and sucked. And now there would be a few more, but on what man or woman weren't they apparent? George felt them all over his body, which he supposed was why humanity had taken to wearing clothes.

'Just do me a favour,' Bernard said.

'Anything.'

'Say nothing about it to Gloria.'

'Of course not. I wouldn't have dreamed of it.'

Bernard put a hand on his shoulder. 'I know you wouldn't.' Then he embraced him, and George felt the hot water of his tears. 'At least she knew I'd be with a friend. I must give her top marks for consideration.'

'Come on, let's spruce ourselves up and get downstairs. We'll take a cab to the Oriental Café, and treat ourselves to the most delicious squid, prawns, and the largest tropical fish on offer. Not to mention a few drinks. We could even split a Peking duck. What say?'

He'd had no further invitation from Gloria, but felt she would have allowed him to sacrifice it. At the flash of her name he couldn't resist reliving the encounter. 'Have you coped?' she said, vibrant from her orgasm, and when he was about to go into her, the much appreciated preliminaries impressing her. Only his experience could have given him so much consideration. He had nothing to cope with, and she was pill-less for whatever reason, so she said: 'What the hell?' And in he went, impossible to think his sperm would take to that extent, yet hoping it would indeed establish itself as confirmation of everlasting love. Either tired of life, or deciding she deserved the luxury of being all of a woman, even at this late hour, she let everything go, a flush of trust and hope not previously known. Whatever was over in her life, let something else begin.

'You have the best bloody ideas of anyone I know.' Bernard chose a clean shirt from the wardrobe. 'And I can't say fairer than that.'

eight

George's small rucksack, brought folded in his luggage all the way from London, leaned against a vacant chair of the next table. 'It's a pity about the weather.'

'Not promising,' Bernard said. Grey clouds were beating up from the south. 'But then, it never was.'

Gloria put a packet of Kleenex into her shoulderbag, and glanced as if there was at last something about Bernard she didn't understand. His musing gaze was set on some spectacle that cut him off from them. George felt her touch under the table, but her features gave no sign of it. She ate a breakfast of bread, cakes and coffee, while he and Bernard set into the usual heavy stuff. 'You'll need more than that if we're to do any walking.'

She was glad Bernard had come halfway back to them. 'I can never eat much in the morning.'

'I expect we'll pick something up at a village cookstall, though my guts have been protesting since our blow-out the other night.'

'Take some more Lomotil,' George told him. 'That should seize you up all right.'

The flesh under his eyes was tender and dark. 'I've chewed about half a pound already.'

Enough paraphernalia lay around them for an expedition, George thought. He'd slept little of the night, lit by a weird dream of an airliner walking on legs back to England, and the frenzied panic of sliding off a cliff. Towards dawn, an idiot repetitive tune wouldn't let him close his eyes, and he didn't know whether he was in pain or not, which uncertainty pushed him into a kind of sleep.

He navigated their rented car while Bernard drove, trying to read the imperfect tourist map. Road signs led them on, then let them down, vanished off the radar screen, and he guided them in diminishing circles around the town centre instead of straight to the bridge as they had hoped.

'A fig for your navigation,' Bernard said.

'You're going too fast in these streets,' she told him.

'Too many motorbikes up my backside.'

George held his pencil to the map, and checked it with a street sign. 'Turn left, then, and take the second right. We'll nip over on the ferry instead.'

The queue of cars and lorries, and a hornet's nest of motorbikes, moved onto a lower deck, the boat soon churning a track towards the mainland. George guarded the right-rear as they joined hundreds of people jostling about the gangways looking for seats or vantage points.

'What are you doing back there?' Bernard called.

'Covering you, tactically speaking, in a crowd like this. Watching your camera. One snip, and you've lost it.'

So he held it in front. 'Let's have a photo, then, to prove we've been here.' Gloria held George's arm. 'And I'll take one of you two old so-and-sos.' They stood by the rail, rain curdling the green water as if at the start of a monsoon, white and grey cloud like a drawing of stomach tripes in an anatomy textbook. The wind's breath was sulphurous and damp. 'Straight out of a sauna,' Bernard said.

'No traps or fishing lines. All done away with,' George said, 'since Kota Libis became a port. No big old sailing junks any more, either, plying a modest trade along the coast. Used to be heaped to the gunwales with sacks and boxes. And those few you do see have motors.'

'A better life for everyone,' she said.

In the old days, the ferry was smaller, and they disembarked via a gangplank straight onto Adam's Pier, the village a few palm-thatched huts for shops, and kampong-style houses among the trees. Now they drove off through a vast super-modern two-storey ferry terminal, a dozen exits going down to various platforms of the bus and train stations. They parked the car to have a look at the place. Avenues on the top floor were given over to cookshops, cake stalls and newspaper kiosks, tables down the middle for people to eat at. 'Who would have believed it?' Bernard said.

Only the old part of Kota Libis was recognizable. The road was muddy under the rain, squalid fences, worn shopfronts decorated with Coca-Cola logos. 'Let's have another snapshot against that Kota Libis sign,' George said, 'as documentary proof that we've been back.'

Gloria stood aside, wanting to get away from traffic and noise, looked at the ferry terminal and tried to figure out the instructions high on the boards for approaching traffic: VAN, MOTOKAR, BAS, BASIKAL, LORI, MOTOBECA, SKEUTAMAAN.

'If I take any more photographs,' Bernard said, dodging waterfilled potholes back to the car, 'I'll be sick. Postcards lie much better than my humble shots ever will.'

So many banks, apartment houses, estate agents, filling stations, secondhand car dealers, workshops and cafés lined the road, making it impossible to guess where the old camp had been, so that they gladly gave up looking for it.

Bernard's face had lost its facility for rapid change of expression, which Gloria accounted for by his having to drive on the right. George knew different, but followed the map, unnecessary because only one road went north: the main artery to Siam. 'Next stop Bangkok?'

'You're goddamned right.' Bernard's fierce response startled her into assuming that something was the matter, which she would like to know about. 'My passport's in the hotel, otherwise it would be home-James for the frontier. I'm serious.'

Palm trees bordered the road, and they slogged on behind a lorry-mountain of coconuts, tyre treads sending gritty water at their windscreen for mile after mile, no hope of overtaking since equal quantities of motorized life crawled from the opposite direction.

Cloud bellies reflected dully into paddy fields from which rice had already been culled. They had nothing to say because the weather and omnivorous traffic seemed to be saying it all. Sungei Patani was drab under the rain, the centre having changed little except for concrete structures which had become old in forty years. Navigation was necessary when they turned inland, the way narrow but still metalled.

There was hardly any traffic. 'Want me to take the wheel?'

Bernard's head was fixed, features unusually calm. 'I've got used to it now. Not tiring at all.'

There must be some good reason why he was not the same person: such absolute change would be slightly alarming if she allowed it to happen to herself. 'I'll drive, if you like.'

'No problem.' His lips hardly moved. Rubber trees, little cups at their trunks, spread back in ranks. 'Not as neat as they used to be.'

'The sun was shining then,' George said.

'Too true.'

'They're not doing too badly, though.' The air of dissatisfaction was obvious, and George tried not to contribute to it. Sorry I got you into it, he would say to her. Not much of an adventure, I'm afraid. Bernard wasn't feeling good, due to gut trouble. I wasn't on top form, either. Don't suppose it was our day. Can't win 'em all, Bernard would remark when they got back.

Well, no. The car didn't leak and they could see the road in front, so what else was justifiably desirable? If one half of him wanted to go back, the other half was full of joy in going on, good to see palm trees and secondary forest to either side of the road. Kids, bright and smart in their uniforms, were crossing the road in a large kampong, their school the only real building.

Gloria stirred in the back. 'It's beautiful scenery. Good to see how the people live in the backwoods.' The road curved, up and down, over the bridge of a watercourse.

'Typical,' Bernard said. 'I knew it hadn't changed.'

'We turn up a track in about two miles,' George said. 'Last time it was unpaved. Take care that you don't miss it.'

'Aye-aye, sir.' In forty-eight the lorries pussyfooted up this road at night with headlights dipped. No, said Bernard, we raced up in daytime, scooting bullock carts out of the way. Intelligence had information on bandit movements infiltrating from the Siamese border zone. That was another time, said George. However it was, the sergeant said: 'We're going to ambush the fucking ambushers.' But with such noise, whether dark or light, everybody had different thoughts. 'A bandit's like a needle in a haystack in this country,' Bernard had shouted in his ear as the plank jumped under them.

'Did I say that?'

'You don't recall it?'

'I remember feeling nothing, not caring or even thinking about making contact, or being killed. Killed! That would have been a laugh. Hadn't a notion what it was all about. I just wanted to get home to my girlfriend, no more high jinks in the house of the five-fingered widow, if you'll pardon the phraseology.'

George joshed that he should keep such terms out of the talk, but she laughed – a good sport, he told himself – and wondered what the equivalent would be for a woman. 'I've never heard the expression before.'

'The dictionaries of slang are full of 'em. Or they ought to be.' Bernard relaxed for a moment into his old smile. A bullock cart came from the opposite direction and they missed its axle by a living inch, the driver twirling his stick as if to beat off an attack of their artful dodger car. 'Right in the middle of the road. What's the insurance on this jalopy? If he'd hit us I'd have killed the idiot.'

'Go slower,' Gloria said. 'It's hardly raining, and I want to see things.'

Trees were painted by bands of moisture. 'Solemn columns,' Bernard said, threading potholes, much splashing as he downed gear. The way straightened and clouds divided, ragged at the edges as if manoeuvring for a battle.

George acted the bomb aimer in a flack-strewn sky. 'There'll be a sharp turn to port. Here it is, steady, steady, bombs away!' No such thing as a signpost, only a gap between the trees. 'Right on the nail. I could never believe we'd find it, but this is it all right.'

'I'm even beginning to recognize it myself.' Bernard drove the car on over red soil, track curving, rubber trees giving way to ordinary vegetation.

Visibility ended a hundred yards away at a wall of leaves and branches. 'It's getting eerie,' she said, such wooded density unknown to her.

Bernard laughed. 'We didn't wend all this way from Blighty for it not to become something. If I'm not mistaken this is what we used to call our element. For forty years we forgot how to live in it, which is why we've gone soft. Or I did. But not any more. Good to get a look at it again.'

George's left arm ached down to his finger ends. The track was occasionally tarmacked, but there were plenty of holes. He wanted to go back to the main road, dismayed to be turning those faded black-and-white photographs into a dull green canyon. Not that I'm afraid, he said, because I've been here before, when there was danger, but we didn't care, not worse because we didn't know, and if we had we wouldn't have bothered. Even danger can be paradise. Nevertheless there was fear which momentarily he could not fight, but fear of what he had no idea, leading him to suggest that they turn round, now that they had seen it. 'Go back down the coast. The weather seems to be breaking. The temples at Taiping are worth a visit. We might as well make full use of the car.'

To the left, the old Sungei Something-or-other, unnamed on his rudimentary map, though he had known it once, elbowed and flooded over the rocks. 'We aren't at the jump-off point yet.' Bernard made an effort to sound reasonable. 'Four more miles, if I'm not mistaken. I'm watching it on the clock. There was a forestry commission bungalow nearby.'

George didn't want to persist with his idea of going back, and be put down as windy. 'So you do remember?'

'Can I ever forget? Silly not to go all the way now we've come this far.'

As if someone had put cotton across the road, George felt that an invisible barrier had been broken. 'Count me in, then,' he said.

'When weren't we counted? But I knew I could.'

How they loved playing such stupidly portentous games, she thought. Creepers hung between the trees, vegetation intertwining, loving itself, yet scenery too glum to be diverting, and she wondered whether George hadn't been right to suggest a visit to something more human and spectacular. Went to those fabulous temples, her postcards would tell them at work, with these two ex-service chaps. One was my boyfriend – no, she wouldn't let on about that, reaching forward to touch his neck, a contact not missed by Bernard via the back mirror.

Dense greenery clothed the road, headlights catching the high foam of the river. No more tarmac, the car bucked over tree roots, jerking at ridges and boulders. 'We should have hired a jeep,' Bernard said. 'But we won't get stuck. Keep right on to the end of the road, is what I say.'

'Dead snake,' George said.

They ran over it, not even a bump at the tyres.

'Deader now,' Bernard called. Marks on the road, so

traffic used it from time to time. 'Hunting parties, I expect. Or surveyors.'

'Or the Malayan Army,' George said. 'There are still a few bandits starving along the Siamese border. They daren't show themselves any more.'

'We put paid to that,' Bernard said. 'Saved the whole goddamned country from the Red Terror. And why?'

'I'm sure everyone appreciates it,' she smiled.

'But did we save ourselves?'

'You can't have everything.' George waited till he had done with a tricky bit, claggy earth slewing under the fuel tank. 'We didn't think of it. In any case it hardly seemed either necessary, or possible, under the circumstances. If it had been ours to reason why we'd have done nothing.'

'Why should you think about saving yourselves?' Gloria asked. 'You were having fun, weren't you? Or so you've been saying up to now.'

'Looking back on it, I rather think someone was having fun with us.' The more flippant Bernard sounded the more George knew he had thought seriously about what he was saying. 'We were having fun all our lives, dancing up and down like silly little figures at a funfair.'

'Having fun,' George said, after a silence, 'gets you doing the stupidest things.'

'I can't think that duty of any sort is stupid,' she said.

He liked that, because she was right. 'I didn't say so. I'd do it all again if I had to. Even then I believed in what I was doing.'

'So you did have thought processes?' Bernard played footsy with the pedals to skirt a rock, skidded, stopped an inch from a tree. The car stalled. 'I caught you out, you dark horse.'

'It didn't do to admit it,' George said. 'Not in those days.'

'They were good times,' Bernard said. 'But we didn't need to talk. Everything was obvious for all to see. Not like the "let it all hang out" brigade these days. We've lived too long for that.'

'Not that long, surely?' she said.

George folded the map small enough to pack into his shirt pocket. He didn't want Bernard, in his present state, to think they were against him. 'They were good times, no doubt about that.' He had spent his life telling children that they should always talk rather than not, persuading them that to express themselves and communicate freely with each other was good, that they weren't thinking unless they verbalized what was in their minds, either in speech or on paper. At one time he had half the children in the class writing letters to the other half, but the headmaster crushed the scheme on discovering that some of the liaisons between the boys and girls had taken a scandalous turn. George saw that he had been successful in getting them to do what for him was impossible, proving that you could pass on to others what you were not able to do yourself.

Bernard was as sharp-eyed now as then. 'There's the bungalow.'

'I don't see it.'

'Across the stream. Near the trees.' The track ended with sufficient space to turn the car, but Bernard left it facing the forest. He got out to stretch his arms, and undergo a stint of deep breathing in the damp air.

George held the seat forward so that she could get out. 'Seems we're here.'

The bottleneck of the clearing was divided by the cutting of the stream, a footbridge leading to the bungalow, where the jungle was claiming its Darwinian rights. Out through the collapsed roof grew a tree, festooned with ivy and laced with creepers, rubble and tin sheeting visible in the crumbled doorway. 'Not much shelter there,' she said.

'Nor anywhere,' Bernard decided, 'by the look of things.'

'We slept in the undergrowth in those days.'

'Like babes in the wood,' she said.

'On groundsheets,' Bernard pronounced, 'after slogging all day through the thick stuff, footsore, weary, and soaked to the skin.'

'Better not shoot too much of a line,' George said.

The pallid, putty-tinted ruggedness taken on during the last few days flushed into purple. 'I've never boasted in my life. You'll see. Say no more. We'll soon get the taste of it back.'

George pulled out his rucksack, slammed the car doors. 'Wouldn't even put my big toe in that lot. All I want to do is eat.'

Gloria stood aside at Bernard's loss of temper, or whatever it was, a strange mood at least, his fingers twitching into a peculiar rhythm, snapping sounds drowned by water hitting rocks downstream. He came towards them with his normal smile. 'Far be it from me not to join in a little refreshment.'

She sopped water from the car bonnet with a bunch of tissues, and laid out the packed lunches wondering what she was doing in so dismal a place. The island beaches were preferable, raining or not, but here she was, and she had been brought up to join in what others seemed to enjoy no matter how different her opinion might be.

Holding bread and a haunch of chicken, Bernard strolled to the footbridge and contemplated the wall of forest.

'Something's wrong with him. What is it?' She stood close to George, and her look into his eyes asked only that he speak the truth.

He kissed her. 'I swore not to say.'

Her eyes were sparkling, as if she was curious about everyone and everything, at the same time showing an intelligent consideration for those whose plight was a shade worse than her own. Her greyish pale hair frizzed out from a lambent forehead, a woman any man would want to go to bed with yet might think twice about should the opportunity come, though he'd had no option, because her lips were the sort he must have seen on opening his eyes after being born, though his mother had been nothing like Gloria. Pictures from the past came vividly today, and he couldn't say why: she was a small slim woman in the dark dress of an apron but for the frock at Christmas and birthdays. He remembered her as worried eternally, though he could never decide what about, except perhaps at the harsh scrutiny of his father whose features exhibited similar grim care in setting the world at a distance from his family – a valid form of love indeed now that he thought of him.

'Is it so serious?' she asked.

He indicated by a touch of the elbow that they walk towards the trees. 'We went into the forest from here,' he said loudly, 'but Bernard swears it was from over the bridge. Even so, it's holy ground we stand on.' Then he resumed, less distinctly: 'He received what we used to call a "Dear John" letter.'

'Whatever's that?'

'A classic blow.' He told her. 'It's knocked him for six.'

'I'm not surprised.' She ate, as if not tasting her food. 'I knew something was wrong, as soon as he sat down to breakfast. A lot went through my mind, but not that.'

His hand stroked her back at the pleasure of being close. 'We've got to take care of him. Be kind, I suppose. Put up with it sort of thing. I've known him for forty years, and realize I know very little about him. Yet I love him, for all that.'

'I think we don't know anybody until we see what they actually do. People in a normal everyday living state are cyphers. He's holding it in pretty well,' she said, when he came back with more to eat. They would finish their meal, get in the car, and go back, having seen exactly what they had come for. Killed the ghost of the past, she supposed, and found nothing to it, tourists, instead of soldiers at the end of their tether.

'Better than the old tinned meat-and-vegetable stew.' Bernard scooped saffron rice from a container with a plastic spoon, and opened a bottle of beer.

'Do you remember those hardtack biscuits we had to hold under water for five minutes before our milk teeth would sink into them?'

Bernard hit him on the back, a wild laugh. 'K-rations!'

'Steady on, or I'll choke.'

'But we got the bandits.' He sent out a spray of rice. 'Walked right into us.'

She stood aside, and let them fool around. They were not, she decided, a pretty sight together, but then, men never were, playing their games as if no one else was close – an obliviousness however that she almost envied.

'Six killed,' George said. 'Two of them women. Pamphlets all over the bushes. A paper war, but we used bullets. Still, we wouldn't have been here now if we hadn't. It was us or them.'

'They had guns as well,' Bernard said. 'Rusty old fowling pieces, most of them.' He was gloomy again, silence insupportable. Someone had to talk above the intimidating rush of water.

'Russian rifles,' George recalled. 'And the bullets were real, as we well knew.'

'Don't know why we had to kill the poor bastards.' Bernard stood at the dark wall of trees. 'There's always good and bad on both sides.' So his barrister father had often said. 'Still, you're as right as ever, George. It was us or them, so we made it them.' He kicked the tyre of the car. 'Then we had to run like hell because the Brylcreem Boys decided to fly in with their bloody great Lincolns, pouring bombs onto empty jungle. I thought our number was up. Don't suppose we should talk like this though in front of Gloria.'

'I'm sure my father would have done the same.'

'You bet he would. And I expect he put a few pointed questions to our prisoners,' Bernard went on, 'after army intelligence had finished with them.'

George had tried to hide it for much of his life:

'You were in Malaya?' he was asked, by young bloods

in the common room, and sometimes by the children.

'Yes.'

'During the Emergency?'

'Just a bit, at the beginning.'

In the sixties he added a little more, for the benefit of earnest Marxists. 'Sat on my arse in the Orderly Room, hoping the bandits might win.' But he had done his stuff with the rest of them, and now the sixties were long since over, reality back in control – for what it was worth.

'You were in Malaya?'

'Yes.'

'During the Emergency?'

'A bit, at the beginning.'

'Must have been tough.'

'Not really.'

'Even so.'

'Oh, I just happened to be there.'

'You saw action?'

He would smile. 'A few walks in the jungle.'

'Still, you were there.' An unmistakable timbre of respect, if not envy, which was puzzling, but it eventually provided him with some gratification at the fact that he had at least been somewhere, not exactly with the Fourteenth Army in Burma, because he had been too young for that, but to Malaya, where he had done a few stunt-like patrols before his number came up for the Blighty Boat. He did not feel ashamed at what he had done, as much as embarrassed that what he had done should become a subject for admiring comment. Better to be merely yourself, and at the same time unrecognizable as anyone in particular, though if he really thought so why had he kept up his association with Bernard, which had always been enlivened by yarning about their time in Malaya? Perhaps a friendship that asked no questions was a blessed state, in a life which for George had been one whole question. 'I'd take it easy, if I were you,' he said, when Bernard poured whisky into his beaker of beer.

'Why the hell should I?'

'Who's going to drive us back?'

She stepped between them, sensing wrongly that they were about to quarrel. 'I suppose I'll have to. As far as I'm concerned, you two silly so-and-sos can get pissed out of your loony minds. Fancy getting sentimental and guilty just because you mopped up a few benighted terrorists! What's the world coming to?'

The claymore of common sense cut them back to as normal a state as they were ever likely to inhabit, welcomed by George who felt he had muddled into saying daft things. 'Go on like that,' Bernard said to her, 'and I'll have to ask you to marry me.'

She smiled, not supposed to know, but touched his arm and said: 'You're married already.'

'So I am. You don't know how lucky you are.' A screeching monkey laugh sounded from the trees. 'Won you and lost you in the same breath. It was ever thus with me, as I suppose some damned poet often said.'

She glanced into the forest, as if hidden ears might be listening. 'I like you,' she said, turning back to them. 'But I love George.'

'I know.' A couple of gold and purple butterflies wavered by. He put out his hand, failed to catch one. 'Lucky man.'

'Who can say?' she wondered.

Well, he said to himself, snapping the head off a brilliant blue convolvulus. I wouldn't marry you, not for a sack of walnuts in a famine. 'Lucky you, then.'

They stood close, eating in silence. The mountain grumbled with thunder like a tiger in a nightmare from overfeeding. George noticed a radio mast on a spur which they had climbed where no human feet were supposed to have been. Bernard strolled to the bank, walked to the middle, and fell between two stepping stones, in up to his knees, his sandwich floating.

'That must take you back a year or two!' George felt

inexplicably happy. She had said she loved him, but so casually that his heart hadn't stopped at such a declaration. The love couldn't last, didn't know why he thought so, not that she knew it, wouldn't believe him if he told her, though in England he would call on his GP to see if anything was wrong with his heart. 'Sound as a bell. Don't waste my time.' At least he would know. In any case he would mention it when they got back to the hotel. I've had twinges coming and going for weeks, it must mean something, indigestion most likely. I didn't go to a doctor because what the hell? If I've had it at least I'll go out with a bang, happy enough for it to happen whenever it likes, because no one has had a fuller life, and if a few years are clipped off, what's that compared to when the lights fuse and you go into blackness without end?

'Bernard's like a kid at the seaside.' She held his arm. 'Men never grow up.'

'And what state might "grown up" be? I've never felt a day over twenty-five.'

She mused. 'I can understand that.'

'Can you?'

Yes, she could. He believed her, otherwise she would not have been drawn to him. Her kiss was brief, but warm. 'You're right,' she said. 'I don't want life to pass me by any more. Even the jungle has a kind of beauty.'

He thought of his marriage. 'I wonder.'

She stared at the greenery, nearer to them because there was no river between. 'I'm inexperienced on that front.'

The rank air drew out his cold sweat. 'The jungle's just a damned uncomfortable inconvenience. But I wanted a last quick look.'

'So did Bernard,' she said. 'Pretty infantile, if you think about it.' They turned, to the splintering noise of water, livid green, a few rocks showing, trunks of the nearest trees smooth and tobacco brown, tall grass between. 'But where is he?'

To get into the forest would be to work your way through a wall. He couldn't remember how they had done it years ago. Just gone in. On this spot someone had taken a photograph, himself in the rear rank wearing bush hat, laden with square pack and rifle, a diffusing grin because his face moved at the click of the camera. In single file they had gone into the dark. But how had they broken the barrier?

They just had. Bernard had repeated the trick, by himself, nowhere to be seen, gone forever out of every life but his own. 'This is all we need,' she said.

'You can hardly blame him, coming all this way. He's only having a look. I might do the same.'

They called his name, voices strangulated by the heavy atmosphere. Their cries were futile. Tumbling water, the odd screech of something or other, a rattle of thundersticks, so how could their pleas be picked up in several thousand square miles of solid forest? Even the walkie-talkie radio had been all but useless most of the time. 'Of course he can't hear us,' she said. 'Let's be sensible, and finish our lunch.'

Bernard would find it easy enough to get out. With such trees and undergrowth you had to climb a good way before losing the noise of water as a guide. And to get out you simply scrambled back to the stream and followed it down. Bernard knew that as well as anybody. He was strong and competent, and in any case he had been here before.

'What about wild animals?'

He smoked his cigar, simulating unconcern. Bernard was true to type in acting the fool. 'There are tigers, snakes, wild boar, buffaloes maybe, but they're sensible, and flee from the presence of man. The jungle's relatively harmless, believe it or not. Drinking water's the problem, but only when you go away from the watercourses. All we saw as we hacked our way through was the back of the bloke in front.'

They cleared the bonnet of food and sat inside, a monsoon hammering at the roof. He'll get soaked, sink into exhaustion, turn delirious, shoot out of his bloody mind. Nonsense. He's a lovable old soldier having a final look-see.

'So you say. Don't you think we'd better search for him?'

'I wouldn't bother,' he said. 'He'll be hard to find, unless he's hoping for it. Even then it might be impossible. I can't imagine what his game is. I can understand him wanting to vanish from the world for a while and lick his wounds, however, and if that's so I'm sure he'll soon come round to thinking it would be better to lick them in a cosy hotel. He's always been one for ease and comfort, has our Bernard, so I expect he'll be back soon enough, drenched but happy.'

'Maybe he's in the mood to let himself in for more discomfort than we can imagine.' She leaned against him. 'Frankly, I'm worried. It's nearly two o'clock.'

He was even more so, and it seemed inevitable that he would have to look for him. Perhaps Bernard wouldn't come out till he had done so, as proof that someone, no matter how insignificant, still cared.

'I fear you're right,' she said. 'The rain's not so bad now. Let's see what we can do.'

His heart was knocking, a sharp stitch from top to bottom. He put an arm over her shoulder. 'Not yet.'

Gentle rain pattered the tin, from clouds which could take their time because they had plenty more on offer, so homely a rhythm washing against the nest they had found. A shimmering curtain down the windscreen was coloured by a reflection of green from the forest. He was afraid of turning on the wipers to see the world clearly lest the batteries wore out and the car wouldn't start. Then, Bernard or not, they would slog ten miles down the muddy track to the nearest village.

The glass was dimmed inside also, by the mist of their breath, a touch of their lips, nothing more worthwhile in this inviolate bubble of their existence, where no troubles infiltrated the protective plexiglass. Her breath was sweet and warm, flesh at the neck smooth, lips moving when they came for more kisses. She shared his happiness, wished they need never move from such shelter. She didn't want to, but stirred, as he knew she must, as both had to, her movements more positive because she took on his conscience as well, and forced him to obey.

'We have to find him.' She opened the door, inwardly railing at Bernard for the disturbance, though without him and his untimely vanishing they would not have been so wonderfully alone.

'At least I have boots on, and long trousers,' he said decisively. 'You'll be all right in the car. I shan't be long.'

His proposal made sense, so why argue? But she thought that if he went alone she would never see him again. He had said that the jungle was harmless, and now he implied that it wasn't. Foolish of him to imagine he could deceive her, and hardly just that he should want to.

He opened his pack, put on a green rain cape, and tied a plastic hat on under his chin. She fell back laughing against the car, at the yellow alarm whistle around his neck. So efficiently clad, he looked forlorn. 'Don't move until I get my camera. I really love you. You look like a fish in all this water.'

She sighted it on a tree, while he lit a cigar, to appear the fearless jungle-basher, giving time for a vertical and a horizontal shot.

'Now we can go,' she said.

'I'm dressed for it. You'll get washed away.'

'I'm soaked already.'

'Your shoes aren't suitable.'

'They're solid enough.' Let him go. He knew the ropes. Maybe they had arranged it between them, to have a last frolic in the playpen of yesteryear. She couldn't in any case see herself wallowing through all that dull and senseless vegetation. And as for them, they were both of a fitness that made them indestructible. But she said, not particularly knowing why: 'Don't go, George.'

He smiled, so that she wouldn't know how seriously to take him. 'I love you, you know that, but I still reserve the right to go to perdition in my own way!' From the bridge he called: 'I'll be back in half an hour. One is just as good as two on this kind of stunt.'

nine

Even better. Far more mobile. The grass was heavy with water, globules jumping onto his trousers so that he imagined a drier trail behind as he walked towards the bank of earth up which he pulled himself by a creeper coming from the branches of a giant tree.

Bernard was right, George following his track of long ago, stumbling between roots as high as his waist, under creepers and lianas, grass hiding the uneven earth. A few more yards, and the dim familiar dankness was all around, neither black-and-white nor Technicolor, became then and now, the past blending into the present, every moment costing breathlessness and sweat.

He went forward, parting the bushes, pulling himself up the soily tangle, the way as steep as it had ever been. To shout would be ridiculous. He couldn't see more than the next trunk enlaced by empires of ivy, the soil soft under his boots. Rain floated and flaked whitely from the foliage that formed an imperfect roof at the treetops.

He whistled the Halleluja Chorus, till his lips became soundless from the rain. Bernard, he said, show your face, for God's sake, an inward pleading so intense that Bernard could not but hear and take notice. Peering in all directions was useless. He scoured for footmarks, broken twigs, signs that nature had not made. Oh yes, in spite of the time-lag, he knew his jungle, glad to be back, I've missed you all these years, happy in a different way to when in bed with Gloria or sitting with her for those sublime moments in the car. That quintessential self he was born with and would die with was familiar at last, a neutral self neither loved nor hated by him, but the competent complacent jungle self who had survived so far and would go with spirit untampered into the dark when the time came.

He called for Gloria, and Bernard would hear her name as clear as his own, but the sound didn't bounce, perished in the dullness. In the jungle no direction was obtainable from sun or stars, you had to manage without sky, only the flow of water to help. He shouted again, heart racked with striving for light and air in the sloping forest.

On a large diamond leaf a brown lace drew itself along, minute and in a way beautiful, a miracle, little more than an inch, a straight line of bloodsucking life that suddenly took the shape of an omega, then turned into an upright line of half its length to get more strength for the onward push towards the treasure island of himself, then a straight line, then forming another omega, and on and on in his direction. Oh you little bleeder if you latch your life force onto me I'll burn your red bag of an arse off with the hot end of my cigar. He laughed as he pulled himself up, recollecting that 'We used to burn quite a few when we stripped at the end of the day. Did us some good, I suppose, in bleeding us like the quacks of old.'

He recalled also that a stream ran by a colliery where he dipped the white cup of a net on the end of a cane for minnows. They darted like splinters of glass, in and out of shimmering weeds, living from cradle to grave in the awesome aquatic cold, unless one came the way of all fish into his jamjar. In a byway where the water lost its power, below a muddy bank, he saw the first leech. 'A bloodsucker,' his brother said. A robust confident brown bloodbag glided along at mud level with a purpose that made him shudder.

'If it gets on you it'll suck you dead.' But you insinuated your way into life through all its terrors, and found that you could live with them.

Rain plopped so rapidly that he could no longer hear the stream, though it was surely somewhere below. But what, he thought, is a superannuated civilian like me doing in such a mire? He sat on the perfect seat of a tree root, and finished a bar of survival chocolate in two bites. Bernard, oh Bernard, when to shout was an effort for lack of breath, why did you drag me into your slough of despond?

Moving parallel to the stream, he drilled the old lectures back, but it was, even so, up and down work, yanking himself across re-entrants and over spurs, miniature as they would have been if not covered by forest. At first he used two hands to pull along by tendrils and roots, but his left arm began to lose power, so he relied more on the right. What necessity such a tangle? Civilization should reap it level, or fence it off.

Bubbles distorted his watch. He wiped the glass with a handkerchief: an hour on his errand. Impossible to know what distance he had come, travel measured in days not miles. He stood, and listened to the dull rush of the stream through the trees, knowing that with the noise of water he was not lost.

He could talk aloud and no one think him mad, another freedom the jungle gave when you were alone, which he was for the first time, because in the old days your oppos were always around or to left and right, though dead silence was the stern command ('So that you can hear the leeches drop off when they've had their little bellies full,' Hollingsworth said) the world you had always known was with you. But now it was silence, in yourself and from you alone, and he knew at last that such silence was out of order – trousers coldly poulticing his legs, boots letting watery mud to his skin, heels rubbed sore – his silence so awful because it was the final rebellion against God, denying all goodness and life.

Thorns scratched his hands. Churning the topsoil on his descent he didn't know where he would meet the river's course, no sergeant with nurtured instinct, or military map and compass to guide. A snag at his cape sent water like cold electricity to his chest. Now the right arm felt less than futile, as if both were two batteries in the same machine that could no longer feed their reserves to each other.

He rested. You don't find anyone by searching, who did not want to be found, but only by luck, Fate pushing behind, or that crooked old finger of Jehovah beckoning from in front.

His limbs ached, so he had to get up and continue the descent in case he fell into the way of never moving again. Rain stopped, rarely any warning of its intent, a sudden full tap and as suddenly the tap was off, the only slow moisture that which collected in the canopies. He peered intently, every second hoping to see Bernard, a damned villain smiling from between the bushes.

He went on his way with as much noise as his failing energy could provide, after seeing a snake's tail vanish from around a branch, bringing back the gaudy cigarette-card memory of snakes-and-ladders played with his brother in the unheated winter attic as a child. Up ladders for luck and down snakes for doom: the only game his father would allow, and even then not on Sundays.

What a way to end, he laughed as the pain struck his heart, stopped, afraid to sit, imagined a terrorist bullet had got him, then after a timeless wait for one thing or the other, went on more slowly, one of the walking wounded, if wounded he was, aluminium sparks playing before his eyes, showing a bigger light ahead, which he must reach, active again in his calculation of footsteps, and for having a six-figure map reference objective that might or might not pinpoint his blackout.

Believe nothing till it happens, and by then if it's your demise with a stencilled number on it, too bad. The only thing left to do was swear, which helped. He took off his cape, got rid of its hindrance and protection, green pieces caught on a bush. How many years before it was indistinguishable from the mulch? A fallen branch squelched into two pieces as his boot went through the crust of bark, an illustration as to how his body would rot if he gave in to the bliss of exhaustion. Daytime denied the luxury of sleep, though he could fall just as easily in the dark. Trees lined up left and right were no longer an unbroken mass, except that another wall began beyond the narrow valley of the stream.

Slowing the pace, he soundlessly insinuated himself, knowing where and how to part the creepers, using both hands in his stealth, and making progress as in the olden days. He wondered what hungry demi-god of the mountain had lured the bandits, members of the Malayan Peoples Anti-British Army, no less, into the gully of this watercourse? En route to terrorize plantation workers into donating food and money, they fatally eschewed all tactical know-how, by failing to send out skirmishers or crown the heights. But the sergeant, wise from the slums of London, deployed the platoon along both sides of the stream. They had played the same game, starting as equals in craft and armament, the sense of purpose high in each, so who could complain? He spat out the bile of guilt, for in any game one side was bound to lose.

Outlandish being here, nonetheless. Hard to take it in. At nineteen, no questions asked, he lived in paradise though he didn't know it. It can't be paradise if you do. Once he got used to duty he was in Eden, England's green and pleasant outpost of a jungle to play at chasing bandits in. But I can't get back to it, he thought, even though here I am, and every passing moment won't return.

Headlands almost met at slabs of rock, the stream in a hurry of white foam to reach the ease of flat land. He craved a rifle and fifty pounds, and into view to appear, sure in their cause, that same band of people also making for the lowlands, Bernard on the opposite bank, peering between vegetation and ready to give the signal. But an ageing buffoon was about the seem of it, because they themselves would soon be caught in Death's crossfire, no sign as to when it would strike, gone before the bang was heard. It could have happened any moment all through life but hadn't, which thought sent him higher above the stream for another reconnoitring look in case Bernard should after all make himself obvious; because if he – George – couldn't find him, there was no one on this earth who could.

Being one with himself from forty years ago he knew the quality of that delicious ineradicable itch where a leech was sucking, and resisted the call to scratch. She stood on the far bank, naked to the waist, alone and unaware. If he forced his way out of the bushes the water would hide the noise, but he lifted his binoculars for a closer look, the figure ghostly white, caught in the sunlight which suddenly spread through clouds as if to suck up the river.

He cleaned the vapour with a handkerchief from his innermost pocket, took time in refocusing to clarify the vision, and saw the curve of her smallish breasts, wondering what kind of deathly magic had produced this indisputable picture of Gloria before the final cardiac blowout.

She combed her hair, gazing downstream, then turned towards where he stood. He sensed her irritation at looking but not seeing. Clothes and shoulderbag were spread on a rock, and now that the itching of the leech had ceased he recalled how, in a safe zone – half the platoon nevertheless picketed – they had stripped for the hilarious drill of getting the bloodsuckers off, then jumped into the pool for a cleansing swim.

To reach her would mean going upstream and crossing where it was shallow. Hard to say where such dreams and visions came from. If he could weed the jungle out of existence he might get a clear answer, but in the realms of reality you were like the blind white fish in intestinal channels of irrigation, finding your way about as best you could. The only jungle he had cleared, back to the damp earth, was the overgrown garden for the old woman who owned the house he lived in, a garden that had gone wild for twenty years. He had worked happily on days when he wanted to combat the atrophy of his muscles, cut into the grass and ivy yard by yard, uprooted brambles, and dug the ground over. By the time he got back fresh weeds would no doubt have appeared, green and vigorous and ready to resume their old ascendant. Yet he had felt pleasure in pulling out such masses of vegetation and raking it to a heap in the corner of the wall for burning. The dotty old woman thought he had been sent by the council, till he told her he lived upstairs. 'I'm going to Malaya for a holiday next week,' he said.

'Oh, don't go to that horrid place. I lived in Zanzibar for twenty years. Go there!'

The obligation of crossing gave him energy, angling to a possible wading place towards where she had been. Not that he expected to find her, since it had been a fact in his life that paradise was never realized. Sweat mixed with water more and more real on advancing into it. The middle was easier to walk along than struggling through bushes which came to its edge. Swirled at the waist, folded in its swathe, he feared a push, an unexpected nudge of watery malice that would send him over and down. He stepped onto an insecure large stone, but he knew those treacherous surfaces, and planted his boot squarely, no longer top heavy with equipment that would heave him over at the slightest skid.

She dipped her shirt into the water, whipped it against the rock with all her might, laughing at the wet drops pearling around. She was at peace and in love, yet all links severed except with the rush of water and the noise of birds. She spread her skirt in the sun, feeling lost yet safe, a cool breeze at her breasts. Tiredness after the walk upriver left her milky and stimulated, the kind of mood in which she might become intimate with herself.

'You gave me a fright,' she said.

He stepped onto dry land, and she jumped at the apparition. 'I saw you from the other side,' he said. 'I could hardly believe it at first.'

'Have you seen him?'

Hard to get breath, but he wasn't dying after all, which revelation made him laugh at his foolishness in thinking he might have been. 'No sign.'

He felt the touch of her breast when she kissed him, then the nipple cool to his lips. She was fresh and odourless, he rank with exhaustion. Drawn as if by the stimulus of survival, they lay on the smooth rock, a passion of reunion. She wanted as much of him into her, body and spirit, as it was possible to get, an urgency as if time was short either for him or for her, she couldn't say why, not caring at the moment about her own sensations.

It was soon over, his life's milk oozing from her, and she wondered how it was that she'd had to wait so long for such love. Only the animals or birds could have seen, impacted blankets of greenery concealing them from the world. They sat, consciousness joined, bemused by the rush of water, sunlight, tiredness, till he stood up and said, arms indicating both banks of the stream: 'I'm beginning to doubt whether Bernard really is up there.'

She curbed a wave of anger. 'Serve him right if he is. I suppose we'd better get back and alert the police. Maybe they'll be able to find him.'

'They'll need a regiment, at least.' He sat again, soaked and mudstained, wondering how long he and Gloria would be able to stay alive if they never went back.

'You look done in.' She saw him as ashen boned and ghastly, a skullhead. But she also saw him as a young man at the end of his strength.

'It takes a bit of exertion, plodding through that stuff.'

She tried to sound loving, in no way censorious. 'I don't think you should have gone.'

'Well, I had to.'

'Yes, he really left you no option. I came up by the stream, wading at times. A bit wet, that's all.'

If he lay down he would sleep for days. 'Is it far? I couldn't tell.'

'Took me about half an hour.'

'Less than a mile,' he supposed, not wishing to diminish her achievement.

'I slipped on a rock and went my whole length. I had to laugh! Bruised my knee. So I washed my shirt to get the slime off.' She put it on, and the bra in the pocket of her skirt. 'I'll lead, because I know the shallow bits.'

'I can't let you. I've done this sort of thing before.'

She didn't want to witness him feeling his exhausted way. 'You just follow me. And let me take that silly pack. Why did you bring it?'

'It's nothing like what we carried before.' Rations, ammunition, rifle, bedroll, mosquito net. How did we do it, we grammar school boys who somehow ended up in the ranks? Even those who had worked in factories weren't fitter than us.

'You're even crazier than Bernard.'

He was flattered. 'There's hope for me yet. I'm sure you're right.'

She went into the water. 'You aren't old enough for a second childhood. In twenty years, maybe. But I suppose that's what every man lives for, when he no longer feels any ambition.' She needed to concentrate on choosing her way, and so did he, a cramp at his ankles. Oh yes, they had felt such discomfort before. Shifting about in those days had taken exactly the same effort, and they hardly went much faster, but they had youth and unquestioning solidarity on their side. Now he was back, plodding the watercourse in the same old primeval forest, having achieved nothing, as they most of the time didn't then, but his body was still up to the mark, though he wondered whether he ought not to slog back via the bushes and hope for a glimpse of Bernard rather than suffer the ache at his knee joints, water coming swiftly from behind as if to push him face downwards and ferry him helplessly towards the sea.

He stopped. The hypnotic curving flood merged with greenery to either side, the smooth painted walls of a city this way and that, Eden and Gehenna hemming him in, and only God to decide which he was fit for, as his father used to say. A dry rock by the stream was flat enough for a bed. They had lain on them at night like the softest of mattresses. 'I'd like to lie down for a bit. There's no great hurry.'

'Oh for God's sake, let's get moving.' If he stopped he would never get up. Even a young man might falter. She felt halfway done for herself, but pulled at his pack, made him take it off and give it up.

'Afterwards, I'll go up there again to look for him. He's the one we should worry about.' His voice sounded brisk and decisive, to himself. To her it was contaminated with weariness. 'You're coming with me.' She took his hand and drew him along, walking backwards, shaming him into quicker headway. 'At the car we'll think things over.'

Returning to camp, you were scruffy and dead, and so was the sergeant, but he barked: 'March to attention!' And the electricity of life shot up your backbone, and you went in as smart in aspect as when you had gone out. So now he said the same words sharply to himself, and surged forward, soon leaving her behind. Once when a man was done up near the end of the day the sergeant silently lifted the pack from his back, handed his rifle to one man, ammo to another, and told off a third to keep him in view.

She let him go in front, a sway in his walk, aching to share the courage of his inexplicable enterprise. There was much about him she could not understand, which she would love as much as that which was already known about him, though she hoped the uncharted area would diminish in extent, wanting him never to vanish from her sight for as long as he could be enchanted into staying.

He turned a bend in the stream, so she unlooped the pack, thrust in her hand, pulled out a tin of bootpolish, and let it drop into the water. Weeping and laughing, she jettisoned a heavy duty torch, then a black claspknife, a whistle, and a plastic bag of radio batteries. Let the manic jungle part of him be left behind forever. A pair of black boots followed his groundsheet, everything into the water. The stuff was all wet, she would say. It was weighing me down. I'm as done in as you are. She found a flask, a full waterbottle, a packet of cigars – unbelievable – and emptied the lot, littering the river bed with thousands of pounds worth of fines! And I'm doing it, she laughed, me, once the ordinary law-abiding daughter of my father who would have thought it very bad form indeed.

The rucksack she could not discard, folded it into a bundle and clutched its rough buckles to her chest, as if George had become so small that she was at last able to carry him.

Bernard sat by the front wheel in a halo of sunshine, a purple butterfly crossing his contented face and waking him from shallow sleep. He seemed not to feel the menace of Gloria's righteous but saturated shoe: 'Where the hell have you two been? A right pair you are, to go off and leave the car locked with all that food inside. I'm starving.'

'And where the hell were *you*?' Gloria shouted.

'It was a bit inconsiderate, to say the least.' George wanted to rest, but relief at finding him momentarily curbed his exhaustion. 'You went off and didn't tell us, so naturally we set out to look for you.'

'Look?' He stood, innocent and refreshed. 'In all that green fuzz?'

Gloria screamed with rage. 'Yes, bloody look. George set out first, and when he didn't come back I went after him. All because of you, you bloody fool. How could you vanish, just like that?' Afraid of attacking him, she walked away.

'You must be off your trollies,' he called, 'to think an old jungle basher like me could be in any danger going for a walk among the trees. I'm buggered if I ever heard anything so outrageously silly.'

George, through whom their currents of insult and injury keenly passed, thought it best to keep silent and let the bad atmosphere disperse. But he said: 'We wanted to find out if you were all right.'

A couple of more selfish snoggers Bernard had yet to come across. George had changed entirely since beginning his holiday affair. 'I've never been so insulted in my life.'

'You've been lucky, then,' Gloria shouted. 'Or spoiled. Or too sheltered. You haven't lived.'

He was bemused, as if she really couldn't be all there. 'Just because I wanted to spend an hour communing with nature, you might say, as any man might . . . You may be interested to know it's not up to much as far as nature is concerned. I'd rather do some orienteering through the Hampshire woods. Imagine you two getting into a panic and thinking you'll come and rescue poor old incompetent Bernard. Well, you can get stuffed, that's all I can say.'

George fetched food from the car, though he had little appetite. He deplored such an end to an interesting day.

'Sorry I shot your head off.' Bernard popped the first bottle of beer, and wrapped his squash-playing hand around a sandwich. 'But you see my point?'

'Blunt as my old auntie's carbuncle, though I'm sure you'd have been worried in my place.'

He smiled. 'That's different. I'd have been up there like a lead weight after the bell.'

Gloria, still sullen and angry, reached for something to eat. 'How the hell did I get into this?' Yet she knew well enough, and wouldn't have been herself if she hadn't.

She took the wheel, and banged the car down the pitted track till Bernard grumbled that the axles would break and then where would they be? 'I don't give a damn,' and her features were set to prove it, though she was so glad to be on the move with everyone safe that she felt like singing. 'If the car drops to bits you can crawl off and spend the night in your precious jungle. Just like in the old days.'

'Lucky it's a Japanese car,' Bernard said, a tree root causing another ominous crack. 'Otherwise it might well be boiled snake for supper.' On the main road army lorries were countermoving north and south. 'A whole bloody division seems to be on the march.'

George stretched out as much as was possible in the back, cocooned in clothing damp from amniotic fluid gone cold. It never took as long to go home as it did to leave home. Homing is quick and painless, unlike the hunger and anguish to reach the point of no return. You departed from the fairy tale base of childhood, controlled by an unconscious yearning for we don't know what, and set out on a journey primed by an energy which makes it seem so easy. Whatever is desired comes gradually within bounds, until suddenly we are in a mire without stepping stones, then a forest without tracks, and endless mountains with impossible alp-like summits, so that one can only hope to keep the mind stable and the body nurtured, meanwhile eternally stoking the human machine for one more effort to reach the timeless paradise beyond the blue horizon where the spirit can exist in peace. Call it Death, though in the last two weeks he had relished something close, joining one time in his life to another to prove that timelessness not time was of the essence.

The light was coming on, but Gloria was bumping the car onto the ferry, a smell of oil and water, vague daylight on opening his eyes, before closing them at pain it wouldn't do to mention. You never complained. People don't like it if you do, neither did he, though if it was a sign of good breeding never to complain it was a sign of even better breeding never to complain of others complaining. Pompous to the last. In any case, those in pain lived in a different world to those who felt nothing. If a pain was serious it would be quickly over, and if it wasn't you would soon have nothing to worry about. He considered the matter from point to point, strange to be so thirsty after plodding downstream, and craving again to view the green after half a day in the raw forest. Wanting to get out and reach water, he touched the door, but his hand fell back at the thought that he must, as his father always said, regret nothing.

'All right, my love?' She was at the wheel, driving back onto the island.

'He's sleeping,' Bernard said. 'I feel pretty knackered myself. It's been a wonderful day, but thank God it's over.'

She would hotspeed it to the hotel and detach herself from Bernard, after making sure he would tip George into bed, where he could stay till he woke no matter how long it took. Her poor bloke needed his sleep. 'It's been bloody murder.'

'I wouldn't say that exactly, eh George?' He wondered what the hell was muddying her bloodstream. 'He's still snoozing.'

The rear mirror was above his level. 'Reach back and wake him,' though she had no idea why she said it so bossily. The wide road behind the museum meant barely another half mile, tree shadows flaking the tarmac.

'You'll never stir old George. I should know. Snores like hell, what's more. I don't suppose you'll like that. He's cutting the forest down, I shouldn't wonder. Amazing how you can hear him above the traffic.'

'Turn and look,' she ordered, sounding, he thought, like her bloody jailer-father. 'And wake him.'

He twisted for a glimpse. Surely it was best to let him sleep. 'Like a babe. Gone from this world. Good old George.'

Her relief was momentary, the smile unreal. Outdoor sort that he was supposed to be, she knew he'd had more than anyone could take, however little some might think it. His expression by the stream had been fixed with a determination to live, but his eyes glowed as if a frightened animal had taken him over, and he realized the grace and favour of how much time was from that moment left. Her love was close to pain at the recollection, seeing his face for the first time in a mirror that had just been cleaned, before the fevered breath distorts and hides.

Pursued by something dreadful, she urged herself through traffic, almost running down a trishaw on the one-way system to the hotel layby. She slammed the door in her misery and fear, stood several yards out on the forecourt and swabbed her damp face with a Kleenex. 'See to George. Wake him, and bring him in.' She tried to smile, sound normal, watched Bernard open the door and prod inside. A couple of Australian officers stared on their way to the row of taxis.

'Come on, sleepy lugs, let's have you. Time for a shower and a drink.' He felt set apart, this no ordinary time, none at all for joking, the words mumbled so that he hardly knew what to say, or what he was saying when he said it. 'We're due for a celebration supper tonight.'

He leaned in, banged his head when coming out and said, as she knew he would: 'It seems he's fainted. Can't tell, though.' Something was worse than all right, as he pulled and pleaded in a tone she hadn't heard before.

Impossible to know how one look told her what had happened. She ran to the reception desk and pushed between a man and woman, new arrivals, handing in their passports. 'Call an ambulance. There's a man outside who's had a heart attack. And for God's sake get moving.'

ten

Empty bottles on the table, Bernard's head was clear, his mind sober. Close to the window, he could hear the senseless beat of water over the parapet, had nothing to say to himself in the stupefying hiatus, sipping rather than drinking, though the bottles didn't seem to empty any slower. Gloria said she would phone, but there had been no call, which might mean good news, but could also signify a situation too appalling to consider. He had always thought George more fit than himself, after a lifetime putting kids through their paces on adventure playgrounds, and leading them across remote mountain plateaux. But a short walk in the Malayan jungle had done for him, because when the heart decides you've had enough it packs in without permission asked or granted. Such turntable thoughts came again and again, words measured by the clock ticking his drift into sleep, head swaying so that the barman hoped he would totter to his room and let him shut down for the night. He shook himself, and called for another beer.

'I wouldn't bother, if I were you,' she said.

'Join me.'

Weariness marked her, a world she had never been in before, half dream, half prophecy realized, torment unendurable – the worst of dreams. 'There's too much to think about.'

'Even more reason. What's the news?'

A hand at her eyes, she took it down, her lips twisted, appalled at her lack of control. 'I have to take his medical insurance papers in in the morning.'

'They're in the room, in his drawer. What's the prognosis?'

'They won't say. Or can't. He's in intensive care.' Shameless, and mortified at having to wipe away tears, she was carrying on as if he was dead.

'He'll live longer than either of us.' He had no hope, either, felt dead and knew he looked the bigger half of it. A friend at the office had come out of a cardiac explosion a new man, but the fan on the ceiling that circled with cheerless inevitability disordered any clear reason to hope. 'George is a survivor,' he went on. 'I've known him a long time. Strong as an ox. He'll be on his feet in a couple of days, raring to get back to the old UK.'

He was as far from the mark as ever, but this time, to judge at least by the wayward flicker of his eyes, he knew it. He was almost as broken as she, but since his moral code – if you could call it that – was only to enjoy life, you could expect no tears, though who could blame him for that?

She wanted him to go on talking nevertheless, which he was well able to do yet not make her aware of the effort. From reassuring words about George, which didn't convince, though both knew that under the circumstances it was the way to speak, he told her of the letter from his wife, and because he had read it so many times sitting in the jungle when they had given him up for lost, and before he had reduced it to the smallest possible pieces, and let it shower like confetti into nature's slowly rotting vegetation, he related the contents in more detail than George had been able to do. She said she was sorry he had suffered such a blow, and admired the way he had not let on about it till now, when he was doing so only to make a tale for her diversion, and acknowledged that he could hardly have done otherwise than go into the forest and be alone. He made her forget her misery in the hour they sat together, and when walking up the wide stairs alone to her room she agreed that there was some reason to hope.

'If you say you can't believe it again,' she said, 'I'll clock you one, I swear to God I will.' They had telephoned from the hospital with the news, the Chinese doctor saying that they had done everything to save him. The earpiece burned to her skin, and she didn't know how much time went by before being able to put it down and go to find Bernard.

Impossible for him to weep, but she cried as if a tree had fallen on her and could never be pulled away. Then through her tears she harried him, and did not consider his loss. He thought of saying much in return, but that would be useless, like arguing with your wife, or the elder sister he would have avoided for twenty years if ever he'd had one. Why the hell did you do it? he said to George. I knew you were a loony. We were loonies together, which was why we never got a commission from King George. 'Too intelligent to be officers,' you used to shout when you were in your ivory-handled mugs, but you might have spared me this final mayhem I had no mind to take part in. Just because I slouched away to think thoughts in the jungle you didn't have to go on a bigger skive and never come back. Was it only so that you could be one more Christian buried in Malaya? Got enough already, I should think.

'I'll give you copies of the photographs I took.' There was damn-all else he could do, in response to her senseless rage in blaming him, but he wouldn't accept that, not on your life, because George, being George's own man, had done what he had to do, nothing more or less, no help from anyone, not even her, so that it was loss all round, loss for her and loss for him, the only gainer being George who had lost so much he had nothing to lose any more, which was a gain if ever there was one, and until that time you had to go on drinking and womanizing even if only to fend off the torments of a life which was hard enough without you yourself gnawing the linings of your stomach. Let her think he was senseless, let her blame him for everything. Did she think she was his wife, for God's sake? God forbid! But he must listen to all such heart-broken ravings in silence if it made her loss one bit easier to bear.

Tears were her words, marking her forlorn face. Poor kid, he thought, when they sat by the terrace the day after the funeral, to have old George by the scruff of the neck (and he had her, too, I'm sure of that) and then to lose him.

'I can't sleep,' she said. In the mortuary parlour, the consul's hand on her shoulder, Bernard on the other side, she half fainted during the final look at George – the white marble-set face, cheeks fallen and lips gone into thinner lines, like someone else whom she had never known but would also never forget. 'Not that I ever could sleep very easily.'

No more continental breakfast, she ate the full house, and he couldn't fault her for that, blessed her for it, in fact, because there seemed little else to bless her for.

'I don't want to get into the habit of taking pills,' she said.

'Why not?' He laughed. 'I swallow them when I need to. You shouldn't be afraid to take advantage of modern science.'

'Oh well, I don't know about that. The doctor at the hospital gave me some. I sleep enough to get by, though. It's amazing what thick dreams come with sleep – mostly about George.'

'Already! Anything interesting?'

Presumably not. Wouldn't say. Clammed up. She would keep everything to herself till the end of time, then take it with her. But to where? You can't take it with you, no more than you can go home again, or enjoy your worldly goods and chattels in the grave. He had dreamed of Jenny, now out of his reach, like George was beyond hers, and beyond his also, everything suddenly far away. The sky was bunged up with strato-cumulus, or some such stuff, George no longer here to put him right on that one.

Their cases were wedded into one load for the long haul home. The airline staff had phoned all necessary calls and tapped with pretty computerizing fingers to get side by side seats and Club Class the whole way. He informed Gloria about the mechanisms that the retiming had been put through, but didn't let on that much smoothing out had been paid for by his credit cards.

The airconditioned car weaved through crowds of happy bikers to the airport, coconut plantations both pretty and exotic, no matter how you looked at it, but as dead at the moment to Bernard as George was dead. Then and now, he wished he had never seen the place. Would the last man on earth think it was beautiful?

He pitied her for the holiday romance which would last a lifetime. At least he hoped so. He sat with the driver, she in the back, and caught her mirrored face, old-maidish with loss, like someone who had escaped from jail, and was being driven back to it after appalling experiences while attempting to get so far that recapture would be impossible. He too was going back, though he didn't mind that, because filling the emptiness would at least be interesting, whereas her empti-ness was still too full, at the moment anyway. He couldn't believe it would be so for ever – that the homing process was a mere drill, movement by numbers and by timetable, that kept her emotions painfully up front. Oh yes, he knew all about it now. Or think I do, he said, but that'll have to be enough for the time being.

An enormous warty knob of cloud rose from a base of other cloud. 'It's George, who wants to say goodbye, if I know him.' Let the dead bury the dead. Ashes to ashes, and all that stuff. The world was empty, but then, it always had been, if you didn't win that ongoing fight to keep it filled. Let her hate me and all she thinks I stand for. George would have felt more or less the same if I had been the one to pop my clogs. One can't become obliterated by the death of a friend, and I have my own way of grieving that she can't know about, or understand if she did.

'You're a clown,' she said, responding to his inane observation, loathing his flippancy.

Suffering deadens the heart, and he was having none of it. The blow of Jenny's letter had prepared him for this one, though without George it was as if his right arm and his left had gone out of the window.

White floss enveloped the airbus. 'We were both clowns,' he said. 'Let's face it.' And when she gripped his arm he wondered if she was showing a mite of friendship at last. Oh Christ, weeping again. Felt like it himself, back to a little boy, the world's misery closing in, didn't know why or what for. Mummy gone out for the evening and left him alone. She couldn't eat her snack, so he took double cakes and coffee for the living, a merry plane of Chinese and Malays, talking and laughing, or fixed by their newspapers.

'You must think I'm a fool.' But she didn't care, more familiar with him than she'd had time to become with George, though without George it would not have been possible.

He sniffed. 'I don't think anyone is a fool. I think more of people than that. Think the best of people, and they won't let you down so easily.'

She couldn't listen, and he didn't mind. 'I only knew him for a week.'

'What's the difference? Forty years or a week, I'm sure they felt the same to George.' Which for the moment was about as kind as he could be. 'I'm dreadfully sorry, for you, even maybe for myself, but in a different way for poor old George.'

He was beginning to talk. Whenever would she? She wept openly, beyond all control, and people nearby looked, as if she had thrown up or something, Bernard thought, not exactly with disapproval, but certainly with surprise. The stewardess brought a glass of water, kind enough to make no remark, though she gargoyled at Bernard, as if he had been married to Gloria for twenty years and he had said the last unsayable devastating phrase which he should have said to Jenny.

She stared into her lap. 'Maybe he's well out of it, with someone like me.'

'That's stupid. You made him very happy. I know him.'

The pilot announced that they were descending towards Singapore, in a voice like that of Peter Lorre. 'It is stupid,' she admitted. 'I'm sorry for making such an exhibition of myself.'

'With good reason.' Hogsbacks of mountains showed through speckled cloud in the distance. There would be a few hours' wait at Changi for a London plane, and he dreaded being with her for so long: coffee drunk in silence, meals left on the plate, magazines worn to a pulp, whisky deadening the senses, then her or maybe both sitting righteous and forlorn in Dubai or some such refuelling dump, as if on the run from having done a murder, shame as strong as grief, features set in wood but guilt bubbling merrily behind.

In normal times, when it didn't matter, he could tell himself that suffering ought not to be endured on one's own. The reality was different. He wanted to be alone, and couldn't remember feeling the need before, but he did not see how he could be, because it was suddenly apparent that there was no more jungle to go into. Perhaps there would be a flower stall at the airport, for no matter how harsh your thoughts, a gesture had to be made. He held her hand during the landing, and in her desolation she did not take it away.

Pargoire l'Herault

June 1989